APR   2008

THE
BILLIONAIRE'S
CAPTIVE BRIDE

THE BILLIONAIRE'S CAPTIVE BRIDE

BY

EMMA DARCY

™ MILLS & BOON®

Pure reading pleasure

First published in Great Britain 2007
Large Print edition 2008
Harlequin Mills & Boon Limited,
Eton House, 18-24 Paradise Road,
Richmond, Surrey TW9 1SR

© Emma Darcy 2007

ISBN: 978 0 263 20026 3

Set in Times Roman 17¼ on 21 pt.
16-0308-41642

Printed and bound in Great Britain
by Antony Rowe Ltd, Chippenham, Wiltshire

CHAPTER ONE

PETER RAMSEY SAW the traffic controller step out onto the pedestrian crossing, brandishing her stop sign, and slowed his car to a halt. A tribe of preschool children, kept in check by a couple of adults, were lined up on the sidewalk, waiting for it to be safe before heading over to the park on the other side of the road. They were all carrying lunch boxes.

Nice day for a picnic in the park, Peter thought, smiling at the happy little faces.

"Nice car!"

The appreciative comment from the traffic controller snapped his attention back to her. She had a wide infectious smile on her face, bright eyes dancing teasingly at him. *Macho male in his BMW Z4 sports convertible being stopped for a pack of kids.* She was enjoying her moment of power. Peter grinned back. *I don't mind, babe.*

She turned aside to help shepherd her flock across the road just as Peter registered a buzz of interest in his mind. He liked the look of her. Her jeans hugged a very pertly rounded backside and long shapely legs. She was tall enough to be a good fit with his height. The scooped neck top she wore showed off a small waist and very attractive breasts, fulsome but not too big to be out of proportion with the rest of her figure. She was a babe all right.

He even liked the fact that her hair was pulled up into a ponytail—dark hair, almost black, the tail swishing as her head turned, keeping a watch over the safe passage of the children. She had a pert nose, too, slightly turned up at the end, and rather pixie-like ears, no lobes. Her skin was clear and shiny with good health. He couldn't see any make-up except for the light pink lipstick that matched the pink in her top. No artful attraction about this woman. She was a natural. Mid-twenties? Difficult to tell her age.

The last of the children—a little boy—grabbed her free hand as though it was a highly prized connection, determined on pulling her along with him. *I don't blame you, kid,* Peter thought, noticing how the boy looked adoringly at her, which probably meant she was one of the teachers from the preschool, briefly taking on traffic control.

She turned to look straight at Peter again, flashing the lovely wide smile as she waved her Stop sign in a cheeky salute to his patience. He raised his own hand in response, his mouth automatically curving as he had the weird sense of a fountain of pleasure bursting through him. He watched her accompany the little boy to the sidewalk on the park side of the road, wanting to follow her, meet her properly.

A car horn beeped behind him.

He drove on reluctantly, telling himself the impulse was stupid. What would a preschool teacher have in common with him? It flashed through his mind that Princess Diana had worked with preschool children before she married Prince Charles. Their marriage might have gone bad but Diana had become the Queen of Hearts. She'd reached out to people, touched them…

What woman had really touched him in recent years? Peter Ramsey, most eligible bachelor in Sydney, heir to billions and billionaire in his own right, and all too familiar with why he could have his pick of beautiful women. Which was fine for his sex life, but he had never been touched deeply enough for any attachment to last beyond an initial rush of lust. Maybe it was his fault. Maybe he had become too cynical about how much he was worth when it came to marriage.

Even the babe with the ponytail…had she smiled at him because of the car he was driving?

Great smile.

The buzz of interest lingered.

Take a second look, it said. *You've got the time. And the inclination.*

After the deceitful artfulness of Alicia Hemmings—his recent ex—it would be…refreshing…exciting…to have a woman without any artifice responding to him. Especially in bed. No faking it with an eye to feathering her own nest. Smiling that lovely smile afterwards…

Even while mentally mocking what was probably sheer fantasy, Peter turned his car into the next side street, spotted a parking space and took it. A quick button-press and the convertible hood lifted back in position for secure locking up. Preferring not to be connected to the driver of the BMW, he removed his cap, sunglasses, jacket, tie, undid the neck buttons on his shirt, rolled up his sleeves, then stepped out for an idle stroll through the park.

It was possible he could be recognised as Peter Ramsey, given his high media profile, but who would believe it when he was so out of place? Besides, it didn't matter anyway. The woman would be surrounded by children, hardly an appropriate time or place to make himself known to her in any sense. Pursuing this impulse was ridiculous, yet the compulsion to go on, if only to satisfy a niggling sense of curiosity about her, had become irresistible. She *was* different to the usual run of women who peopled his world.

A corner shop provided him with sandwiches and a can of cola and he carried them into the park, feeling as though it would look perfectly reasonable for him to be having his lunch there. In fact, he was enjoying the novelty of it, enjoying the pretend game of being just anyone. Acting on this particular impulse was definitely not boring.

The children were seated on the grass, shaded from the midday sun by the widely spread branches of a Moreton Bay Fig. They were all looking enthralled at the ponytail babe who was apparently telling them a story. Peter settled on a nearby bench seat where he could surreptitiously watch and listen to the story-teller.

Her face was full of animation, very watchable. She also had a voice worth listening to. It lilted beautifully as she recited the rhyming verses of a fairy tale—a charming story about a princess with a magic rainbow smile and a heart of gold who'd come from the land of Evermore to bring joy to all the children.

Of course, there was the villain of the piece—a sneaky kid who always wore black and was really a rat—who set out to spoil every bit of happiness and spread lies about the princess, making her disappear from the children's lives. But one small boy didn't believe the rat's trickery and he cried out in a mighty lion's roar, bringing the princess back from the land of Evermore and exposing the rat for the stinking, rotten liar he was.

Standard stuff—good triumphing over evil—yet Peter was completely captivated by the rhyming verses and the perfectly pitched emotional delivery of them. The pre-schoolers listening so avidly to every word, actually came in on some lines as though they knew much of the story by heart, especially the lion's roar bit. It had tremendous appeal and no doubt came from a popular children's book. Peter decided to look for it, buy it as a gift for his nephew some time in the near future.

Once the last line had been recited, the children clapped and jumped up to form a dancing ring. There was a bit of a scuffle over who got to hold the story-teller's hands. One of the other adults dryly advised, "You'd better be the princess in the middle, Erin."

Erin...

Nice name.

And she was great with the children, all of whom clearly adored her.

He was feeling *very* attracted to this woman, and not just on a physical level, though her sexual appeal was certainly getting stronger by the moment. He imagined her telling him fairy tales in bed...erotic ones...like Sheherazade, keeping her sultan entranced with her stories, making every night too good to miss.

He'd like that.

Very much.

So how was he going to meet Princess Erin in an acceptable fashion?

She could be married for all he knew, or attached to some guy she was in love with. Peter didn't care for that thought one bit, quickly brushing it aside to concentrate on what tactic would give him the result he wanted.

There was no easy *in* here, not like for his friend and now brother-in-law, Damien Wynter, who'd taken one look at Peter's sister and charged straight into getting Charlotte to marry him instead of the fortune-hunter who'd almost had a wedding ring on her finger.

He remembered asking Damien how he knew Charlotte was *the one* for him. The answer was still imprinted on Peter's mind.

"There's a buzz in your brain that tells you not to miss out on what you could have with *this* woman. She fits what you've been waiting for."

Were his instincts telling him that Erin might be *the one?* The mocking voice of past experience said that was jumping too far too fast. Right now he was hooked enough to know he didn't want to walk away from her, shutting a door that might lead to something good, something better than he'd had in the past. No matter how unlikely it was…

"Hey!"

The startled cry of alarm came from one of the teachers as a man charged the circle of dancing children and grabbed one of the little boys, snatching him up in his arms and hugging him tightly against his shoulder.

"He's my son!" he threw at the three women who started toward him, protesting his action. It was like an animal growl, fiercely possessive, and the man backed away, eyeing them wildly, still clutching the boy to his chest.

The women argued with him.

The children started wailing, agitated by the sense of volatile conflict that had so suddenly erupted.

Peter sprang into action, catching snatches of the argument as he circled the Moreton Bay Fig to come around behind the threatening kidnapper.

"I'm his father. I've got every right to take Thomas with me."

"We're responsible for him, Mr Harper. His mother left him with us for the day and…"

"His mother took him from me. He's my son!"

"You need to sort this out with your wife."

"She won't let me have him but she dumps him with you people who are nothing to him. Nothing! I'm his father!"

"We'll have to call the police if you take Thomas."

"Mr Harper, this is not a good move. If you end up in jail, you'll never see your son." That was Erin's voice, gently pleading reason.

A high crazed laugh derided any reasonableness. "There's justice for you. I do nothing wrong but I lose my son and my cheating bitch of a wife just gets him given to her."

"You have to take this to the family court," Erin pressed. "You'll get a fair hearing."

"Nothing's fair!" The exploding anger

cracked into spurts of tears as grief and despair poured from him. "She's told a stack of lies about me to her big-shot lawyer. I've got no chance except this. No chance! You tell my wife she's welcome to her money-bags lover, but taking my son…no…no…no…"

The tortured sobs of the man were gut-wrenching. He was shaking his head, backing away from Erin in a blind stumble.

"I'm calling the police," one of the other teachers said, a cell phone already in her hand.

"Don't!" Peter commanded as he moved in and clamped an arm around the bereft father's heaving shoulders, stopping and supporting him.

Erin lifted a startled gaze to his. "Who are you?" she asked.

She had green eyes.

Beautiful green eyes.

And Peter felt a compelling urge to answer every question in them. Except…he didn't want to throw the weight of his name around with her.

"I'm just a guy who hates to see another man reduced to tears," he said, then shot a look of incisive authority at the teacher with the phone. "Stop that right now. I'll take care of this. Calling in the police will only make everything worse."

"I'm in charge of these children," the woman argued. She was a good deal older than Erin, maybe in her fifties, iron-grey hair cut short, plump figure, and puffing herself up officiously. "I have to answer to Mrs Harper about what happens to Thomas."

"Nothing is going to happen to Thomas," Peter assured her. "Mr Harper just needed to hold his son for a few minutes. Fair enough in the circumstances, wouldn't you say?"

"He has to give him back," the woman insisted.

"Yes. And you can trust me to see that he does. I'm big enough to do it. Okay?"

The man he was holding was too shattered to put up a fight and would have no hope of winning against Peter even if he did pull himself together.

The woman protesting his interference took stock of Peter's height—well over six feet tall—his broad, muscular shoulders and powerful physique, all of which made him a formidable opponent in any arena. Harper was a relatively small man, the top of his head barely reaching Peter's chin, his far more slender frame almost dwarfed in comparison. If it came to physical force, it was obvious who would end up controlling the situation.

"Make him give the boy back now," the woman demanded.

The boy spoke for himself. "I want my daddy. I love my daddy." He flung his little arms around his father's neck and snuggled his head close. "Don't cry, Daddy, I don't like you crying."

Tearing him away from his father would be brutal. There were other, kinder solutions to this situation. "Let's take a bit of time to calm everything down," Peter directed at the woman, trying to engender a spark of sympathy. "I'm going to walk Mr Harper over to that park bench…" He nodded to where he'd seated himself earlier. "He can sit with Thomas while you supervise the other children at play."

"They're all upset now," she protested. "We should take them back to the kindergarten and settle them down."

Peter switched his attention to Erin whom he found looking straight at him, a curious wonder in her lovely, luminous green eyes. Desire hit him hard and fast. Close up to her like this, any lingering doubt about pursuing this woman completely disintegrated. The adrenaline rush in his blood, the tingling in his groin—nothing jaded about these feelings. He wanted her and he was going to have her.

"Tell them another story," he suggested, smiling to push the connection that had to be made. "You're very good at it. I was listening to you while I ate my lunch. I'm sure you can make any trauma fade away."

A twitch of a smile back. "Thank you. I think that's a good idea."

"Erin…" the other woman chided, obviously afraid of consequences with the situation taken completely out of her control.

"He *is* big enough, Sarah," she stated confidently, waving away any further protest.

No rings on her left hand.

"Besides, you can always call the police if things don't turn out right," she added to appease ruffled feathers.

Triumphant pleasure surged through Peter. Erin was on side with him. Whether it was over this issue—fathers who got a raw deal when it came to divorce—or more a positive response to his presence on the scene—the man he was—he didn't know, but a step had been made and he could exploit it.

Erin re-engaged with him, appealing for his co-operation. "We'll have to collect Thomas on our way back to school."

"Understood. Better make it you who does the collecting," he pushed. "Thomas is less likely to cut up rough if he's taken from his dad by the princess."

She had pale creamy skin and it suddenly bloomed with colour. Peter couldn't remember any women of his acquaintance ever blushing. He found it quite entrancing.

"All right," she quickly agreed, then turned away to gather the children into a happy little group again.

The officious Sarah frowned disapprovingly at Peter but she clucked around her flock, not quite prepared to keep fighting his plan but still fretting over being thrust into the position of trusting a stranger. Nevertheless, having to call the police and deal with legal issues was not an attractive idea, either.

Having successfully manoeuvred a second meeting with Erin and won some time for the distressed father and son, Peter virtually scooped Harper along with him to the designated park bench, encouraging his compliance with a spate of sympathetic talk. "I know it's all got on top of you, mate, but just fall in with me now and let's see if we can find a better way to get you back with your son."

There was no fight left in Harper. It seemed to Peter the man was completely at the end of his tether, almost collapsing onto the bench and rocking his little son in a kind of desperate love, having no hope at all for the future. When he was composed enough to speak, he looked at Peter with anguished eyes and said, "She told her lawyer I was an abusive father. It's not true. Not true…"

Peter believed him. Far from showing any fear of his father, Thomas was clinging to him as though he'd missed his dad as much as

Harper had missed his son. The caring was obviously mutual.

"A good lawyer should be able to set that straight," he advised.

"I can't afford one. Lost my job. Couldn't give it the energy it needs…"

"What work do you normally do?"

"Salesman."

"Okay. What if I find you another job, set you up with a lawyer who's an expert on custodial rights, ensure you have the best advice on how to handle what's happening now…"

"Why would you do this?" His eyes reflected confusion, an agitated mixture of uncertainty and mistrust. "You don't even know me."

It made Peter pause for a moment to sift through his motivation. Because a father shouldn't be forcibly separated from his son? Because he hated seeing a man destroyed by a woman who took everything from him? Because of the sheer injustice of what was happening?

Or because impulse was ruling his life today! Erin…

Connecting himself to Thomas's welfare gave him a step into her work-place, a follow-up point for pursuing a connection with her. Harper didn't know it, but he was a heaven sent opportunity for Peter to further his acquaintance with a woman he wanted.

However, the simple answer was, "Because I can. And I want to help you, Harper. I want Thomas to have his father in his life. It's important."

He shook his head in disbelief. "You're promising a hell of a lot."

"Trust me. I can and will deliver on what I'm offering."

A searching look, wanting to believe, hoping for a miracle, then the question… "Who *are* you?"

The same question Erin had asked.

Peter knew he had to answer this time. It

would give instant credence to what he'd promised. He pulled his wallet out of the back pocket of his trousers, opened it and showed Harper his driver's licence for identification.

"Peter Ramsey," the man read. The shock of the well-known billionaire-tag name hit him almost instantaneously. His eyes widened as he stared at the face that had been regularly displayed in the media for years—the squarish jawline, dark blond hair, blue eyes, strong arrowed nose, prominent cheekbones, a sprinkle of freckles from boyhood years in the sun—recognition sinking in. "What are you doing here?" spilled off his tongue.

Alone in a common park without the entourage that usually accompanied his public appearances... Peter shrugged it off. "Just taking a bit of time out of *my* life."

"Like a chance in a million," Harper muttered dazedly.

Which raised an ironic little smile. "Guess your luck was in for once."

"You really mean it? You'll help me like you said?"

"Yes, I will. You can come with me and we'll get things moving in a positive direction for you right after Thomas has to go back to the kindergarten. In the meantime, why don't you have a chat with your son, find out how life has been going for him since you've been separated?"

Harper thrust out his hand. "This is mighty generous of you, Mr Ramsey."

"No problem," Peter assured him, shaking his hand.

"I'm Dave. Dave Harper."

"Good to know you, Dave."

It *was* good—listening to the man reassuring the little boy that Daddy was okay now and they would get to see each other again soon.

Erin was weaving her magic with the kindergarten children, telling them another fairy tale in rhyming verses. Not one of them looked away from her to check on how Thomas was doing with his father. Disturbance over, Peter thought.

Nevertheless, the older woman, Sarah, would undoubtedly feel obliged to report this incident to Thomas's mother when she came to pick him up later this afternoon. Which could cause Dave more grief. Although the kidnapping had been averted, the threat of it could be used against him. Better to fix that possible problem before it got rolling.

Besides, the fixing would give him the chance to meet Erin properly.

He would have to use the power of his name to get past Sarah's objections to his interference, but he couldn't remain incognito with Erin indefinitely anyway. He grimaced over the necessity for his identity to be revealed, knowing it would inevitably be a factor in how much she would want to know him.

It was always a factor.

But right now he didn't care.

The desire to have her was far too strong to care about any other factors.

CHAPTER TWO

WHAT a man!

Part of Erin's mind kept buzzing over him even as she carried through his suggestion of concentrating the children's attention on another story.

A big man in every sense, she decided—strength, compassion, authority, as well as having a fabulous physique emitting so much male power, her female hormones were leaping around in a frenzy of interest. Definitely a prince of a man, and I'd just love to be his princess, she thought dizzily.

She'd caught a glimpse of him strolling through the park earlier and instantly liked what she saw—very impressive. When he'd settled on the bench seat in easy earshot of her story-telling, it had been impossible to resist the impulse to show off to him, pouring much more vitality into her performance than she usually did. Which was really silly because he was an absolute stranger with no chance of their meeting, given that she was caught up with a group of children.

Then had come his amazing intrusion when Thomas's father had been about to make a terrible mistake. Generally people did not involve themselves in problems that were none of their business. Yet this man had, taking firm control of a very scary situation and producing alternative courses of action right off the top of his head, which demonstrated a mind used to cutting through to the heart of the matter in no time flat.

He'd even flummoxed Sarah with his air of commanding authority and Erin had never known Sarah to surrender her own authority to anyone else. It was good that she had on this occasion, though. Thomas's father obviously needed help, not a stint in jail, which would defeat any hope of getting visiting rights with his son. Erin felt sorry for him. Having his wife desert him for a richer man and taking their son with her...he was in a bad place right now.

Apparently Sarah had decided *they* were in a bad place, too. As soon as the story ended, she was urging the children to pick up their lunch-boxes and form a crocodile line, ready for their return to the kindergarten. She picked up the traffic Stop sign herself, and directed Erin to collect Thomas. "And don't be put off by the guy who took them over," she instructed emphatically. "The boy's mother could sue us for negligence."

"I'm sure he'll see that the agreement is kept," Erin replied confidently.

"Didn't your mother ever teach you not to trust a stranger?" Sarah grumbled.

By their actions you shall know them, Erin recited to herself as she set off to approach the big man and the father and son he had taken under his protection. This guy was good. In fact, with his tall, muscular build and thick mass of blond hair, he was the perfect image for a splendid Viking warrior, wielding his powerful sword to fix wrongs. She could already see him being the hero in her next story.

He stood up when he saw her coming. Mr Harper remained seated on the park bench, speaking anxiously to Thomas who was on his lap, soaking up being cuddled by his father.

Erin was conscious of her pulse leaping into a gallop as she met the steady gaze of the self-appointed intermediary. There was a riveting quality about his blue eyes, giving her the weird sensation of a laser-probe straight to her heart.

Her skin tingled as though hit by an electric charge. She'd met a lot of different men in her globe-trotting, literary career. Not one of them had made this kind of impact on her. She wanted to say, "Don't walk out of my life," but such a plea seemed too embarrassingly presumptuous.

"Time to go," she said, feeling a sickening irony in having to act on those words instead.

"It's okay," he assured her. "Your name is Erin, right?"

"Yes." She hesitated, wondering if he would recognise her much published author name and all it now stood for, whether it would mean something positive to him, enough to spark an interest in knowing her. In a self-conscious burst, she added, "Erin Lavelle."

"Lavelle," he repeated, rolling it off his tongue as though tasting it.

But she could see it hadn't made any impact on him. He didn't know of her. He was probably more a man of action than a book person. They were simply passers-by, not occupying the same world, only this bit of park on a summer day.

He smiled, the flash of perfect white teeth reminding her of the smile of the BMW driver, but this couldn't be the same man, could it?

"Sarah is the one in charge of the kinder-garten?" he asked.

"Yes. Sarah Deering. She's my aunt."

Why she'd given this information, she didn't know. It was irrelevant.

"I don't suppose Ms Deering will let this go—not report it to Thomas's mother," he probed.

Erin shook her head. "I think Sarah will feel the need to cover herself in case of a repeat occurrence."

He nodded and handed her a business card. "Tell your aunt I will personally ensure that the right avenues for custody will be pursued." The blue eyes hardened with intimidating purpose as he added, "She might like to pass that on to Mrs Harper."

For some reason he was assuming he spoke from a position of power. In fact, power radiated so strongly from him, a little shiver of trepidation ran down Erin's spine as she glanced at the name on the card.

Peter Ramsey.

It meant nothing to her.

She looked up, frowning her puzzlement. "Who are you? Why do you think this carries some weight?"

Surprise at her ignorance was swiftly followed by twinkles of amusement. "Just show the card to your aunt, Erin. It tends to influence people, believe me."

She heaved a rueful sigh. "Guess I'm out of the general loop."

He grinned. "Charmingly so. May I ask a favour of you?"

"Ask away," she invited, dazzled into ready compliance by the grin that seemed to say he found her attractive, too.

"My cell phone number is on that card. Call me after Mrs Harper has been and gone this afternoon."

Excitement zinged through her. This might not be the end for them. "You want to know how it pans out?"

"I'd like to hear your impressions of the mother's reaction to what happened here." He grimaced. "Truth tends to get lost when it comes to divorce and the best interests of a child are not always served."

"You're right about that," she said with feeling, having been the child of divorced parents herself.

"So you'll call me?" he pressed.

"I will," she promised, blithely uncaring about whether it was appropriate or not. The call might lead to another meeting with this amazing man.

"Good!" Satisfied that a pact had been sealed, he turned to the father and boy. "Got to let Thomas go with Erin now, Dave."

There was no argument.

"I'm sorry for the scene I caused," Mr Harper offered as he handed Thomas over to Erin.

"I hope you have good times together in the future, Mr Harper," she replied with genuine sincerity, then quickly led the boy away, seeing that Sarah had the crocodile line in order and was anxiously waiting for them to join it.

She was incredibly conscious of her body as she walked away from Peter Ramsey. It was as though she could feel him watching her, assessing everything about her. It made her shoulders square up to a straighter carriage, caused her bottom to feel twitchy, and her knees actually threatened to wobble. She didn't look back, telling herself to maintain some dignity and not moon over the man like some star-struck teenager. His card was in her hand. That guaranteed another connection with him.

Once back at the kindergarten, Erin helped settle the children for their afternoon nap. She had intended to leave at this point, having done the favour her aunt had requested. A story-telling session from Erin Lavelle was great PR for the preschool, backing up the much-dropped fact that she was, indeed, Sarah's niece. However, the intriguing encounter in the park demanded a change of plan.

Having taken the precaution of copying the essential details from Peter Ramsey's card into the notebook she always carried with her, Erin slipped into the administrative office to have a private conversation with her aunt who was sitting at her desk, hunched over a newly made cup of coffee and looking as though she needed a shot of caffeine to stitch frayed nerves back together.

"That could have been nasty. Really nasty," she said with a roll of her eyes. "Thanks for helping out, Erin. I don't know how I would have handled it…" Her voice trailed into a heavy sigh as she shook her head over the frightening incident. "The children could have panicked…"

"It was lucky Peter Ramsey was there," Erin quickly put in.

The name jolted Sarah out of her fretful train of thought. Her eyes sharpened to a wary alertness. "Who? Who did you say?"

"The big man. His name is Peter Ramsey. He gave me his business card…" She placed it right in front of the coffee cup, hitching her bottom onto the front edge of the desk's large surface as she explained the card's purpose. "He said for you to mention his name to Mrs Harper if she gets ugly over what her husband did."

Sarah picked up the card and stared at it disbelievingly.

Erin carried on with her job as messenger. "He also gave his personal assurance that Mr Harper would seek legal help to get some custody rights, so you shouldn't be afraid of him going off the rails again because of not being able to see his son."

"Peter Ramsey," her aunt said with almost breathless awe. Her eyes were goggling when she looked up at Erin. "I should have recognised him. But why on earth would he be in that park?"

Erin honed in on the most pertinent point. "Why should you have recognised him?"

"Because of who he is, of course," her aunt brushed off impatiently, then caught Erin's grimace of frustration. "Don't tell me you haven't heard of him. He's Lloyd Ramsey's son and heir."

This stunning revelation was a blow to the fantasy that had been building up in her mind. "You mean the multibillionaire, Lloyd Ramsey?"

"The one and only," her aunt confirmed.

Lloyd Ramsey was virtually an Australian legend, making so many headlines over so many years, even Erin who'd always lived in the world of books, was not ignorant of the man's power and how he wielded his wealth. He'd been nicknamed "the shark" because he went after a bite of just about every big business enterprise going. From Sarah's reaction to Peter's name, apparently his son had also carved out a prominent position in Australia in more recent times.

Erin had the queasy sense he was way out of her league, occupying a far, far different world to hers. "Is Peter Ramsey a business whiz, too?" she asked.

"Very much so on the international scene," came the heart-sinking reply. "All high-tech stuff. I'm not up with that but he's always in the social pages, being photographed with other celebrities. Every time he changes women it's big news."

Erin's stomach did a dive, too. "You mean… he's a playboy."

The macho BMW sports car popped back into her mind. Had he been the driver?

Her aunt shrugged. "Well, he's still playing the field. Hasn't married anyone yet. Probably doesn't give much time to his relationships.

Always on the go. And let's face it, a man in his position can get any woman he wants when he wants."

Yes. He probably could.

The excitement that had been fizzing through Erin's bloodstream completely flattened out. The possibility of Peter Ramsey being *her prince* was looking dim if not downright dead.

Yet he had certainly played knight to the rescue in the park and she *had* felt a strong connection with him. On the other hand, their shared empathy for Mr Harper's situation could have accounted for that feeling, plus, of course, her instinctive response to his very dynamic sexual appeal.

"Why do you think he's involved himself with this?" Erin asked, wanting more input from her aunt.

Sarah shrugged. "Why was he in the park? Maybe the two are connected."

"What do you mean?"

"There must have been a trigger for his action." She paused to think through what had happened. "Maybe he overheard Mr Harper yelling out that he'd been ripped off by his wife. That could have hit a sore spot with Peter Ramsey."

"Do you know that some woman has just ripped him off?"

"No." Sarah leaned back in her chair, a cynical little smile tugging at her mouth. "But it has to be always on the cards with that much wealth on the table. Remember what happened with his sister."

Erin shook her head. "I don't know anything about his sister."

Sarah looked surprised. "The story ran in the media for weeks. It was huge."

"When?"

"Oh—" she waved her hand as though trying to grasp the time element "—must be almost three years ago."

Erin thought back. "I was travelling through Asia then."

"Always off somewhere," Sarah remarked with a sigh of exasperation at her niece's footloose life. "You should stay home more often, Erin."

The cynical thought instantly slid through her mind—*What home?* Her mother had re-married and made a home with her second husband—no room for her daughter. Her father…fat chance of being welcomed for more than an hour or two in his household! The house she'd bought at Byron Bay was her writing base but it was always lonely there, not what a home should mean.

Out loud she said, "So what about Peter Ramsey's sister?"

"Big scandal!" her aunt answered with relish. "Charlotte Ramsey was about to marry one guy and just before the wedding he refused to sign the prenuptial agreement her father had drawn up. She turned around on the spot and married the British billionaire, Damien Wynter, instead. Her former fiancé proceeded to sue for ownership of the apartment they'd shared—hers, of course—in a de facto relationship. He got it, too. Didn't go to court. She signed off on it. The point is…"

"He was in it for a slice of the Ramsey billions."

Sarah tapped the desk with her finger to emphasise the train of reasoning in her mind. "He was going to rip her off."

"And she didn't have that problem with Damien Wynter," Erin concluded. "Which is rather sad when you think about it, finding out you're only being married for your money. I wonder if Charlotte Ramsey is happy with her British billionaire."

"Erin, you might write happy endings for your stories, but there's no way you can guarantee them in true life," her aunt said dryly.

"True. But for whatever reason, Peter Ramsey

seems intent on underwriting a happier ending for Thomas and his father." She raised an appealing eyebrow. "Mind if I stick around to see how Mrs Harper takes that news?"

It drew a curious look. "Why so interested?"

"The power of a name," Erin tossed off casually. "I just want to see it in action."

"She doesn't pick him up until five o'clock."

"That's okay. I'll go for a walk in the meantime."

"Mmm…" Sarah pondered the request. "It might be wise to have a sit-in witness."

"Absolutely," Erin pressed, hopping off the desk and waving a goodbye before her aunt had second thoughts. "See you later."

She didn't walk far. Her feet automatically took her back to the bench-seat Peter Ramsey had occupied in the park. She sat precisely where he had sat, her mind running hot with thoughts about him. He hadn't acted like a playboy. He had seemed serious and caring.

Though she had to admit the serious caring had been directed at a father and his son, both of whom were apparently being short-changed by a woman.

Maybe his attitude towards women fell into an entirely different category. What experiences had shaped the man who had stepped in to make a difference—a positive difference—to a man and boy he didn't even know? Erin knew she was too intrigued to turn her back on learning more of Peter Ramsey. She'd promised to report back to him on Thomas's mother and she would make the call.

If she had imagined a personal interest in herself, he wouldn't set up a further meeting with her. But if she hadn't imagined it…if he did want another face-to-face encounter…a surge of strong resolution tossed caution—or wisdom—aside.

She wanted to be with him.

How many times in her life had she felt like this about a man?

None!

Seize the day, she fiercely told herself.

If she got the chance to seize it.

CHAPTER THREE

"PETER RAMSEY."

His voice held a clipped self-assurance, demanding an efficient reply.

Erin took a deep breath to calm her jiggling heart. Speak to the man. Reach out to him, she told herself. You have this one chance!

"Hi! It's Erin Lavelle." The words spilled out in a breathy rush. Oh great! she thought. He's probably hearing the pant of a gold-digger who hopes she's onto a good thing with this call.

"You do have a very distinctive voice," he said, and it sounded as though he was smiling through the words.

Smiling with pleasure!

A wild, wonderful hope danced through her mind. "You asked me to call," she reminded him.

"It's come later than I expected. I thought you weren't going to contact me. I'm glad you have."

It *was* pleasure. Warm pleasure. A smile burst across Erin's face. "Mrs Harper didn't come until five o'clock. She's only just left."

"Ah!" The sound of satisfaction. "There must be a lot to tell me and I do want to know all of it. Would you join me for dinner, Erin? I've been with Dave Harper most of the afternoon, getting his side of the story to a good lawyer. I need to hear your impressions of his wife."

"Dinner…" she repeated dazedly. The invitation had come so fast her head was spinning.

"Regardless of what people might have told you about me since our meeting in the park, I promise I'm not the big bad wolf, and you don't have to fear my gobbling you up on the spot," he assured her with dry mockery.

"Right!" she said, though the idea of being

gobbled up by Peter Ramsey had actually sent her pulse-rate zooming. "Where and when?" she asked, trying to sound efficient and not too eager.

"Whatever suits you, Erin."

Which lobbed the ball straight into her court.

Was it a test of how much she would try to screw out of him?

What did he expect her to choose?

Best to go for her own comfort zone, she swiftly decided, given she was in an absolute tizz about meeting him again. The intimidation of a ritzy restaurant would only make her more nervy.

"Are you okay with a downmarket place?" she asked, wondering if he preferred the privileges that went with being recognised in trendy surroundings.

"No problem," he assured her.

So he didn't need ego-stroking.

"Do you like Thai food?"

"Fine with me."

He was being very accommodating.

Glowing happily, Erin gave directions. "Along Oxford Street, between the end of Hyde Park and Taylor Square, there's a little restaurant called Titanic Thai. I could meet you there at seven-thirty."

"Should I book a table?"

"No. I'll drop in and ask them to keep me one."

"You live nearby?"

"More or less," she answered vaguely, not wanting to divulge too much about herself at this point. "I'll see you there then?"

"Seven-thirty, Oxford Street, a Thai restaurant called Titanic but it's only little," he said in a tone of amusement.

"That's it," she confirmed and rang off, feeling pleased with herself for not only seizing the chance he'd held out, but for taking command of proceedings, as well.

Her feet wanted to skip all the way to the bus stop.

* * *

Got her!

Peter's hand clenched in exhilarating triumph.

Then he laughed at himself for being so absurdly excited over another meeting with a woman whose life was so remote from his, they'd probably have nothing to talk about apart from Dave Harper's miserable situation.

Nevertheless, that bit of reality did not dim his desire to experience all there was to know of Erin Lavelle. He'd been in the mood to embrace the wildly improbable ever since she'd smiled at him at the pedestrian crossing, and tonight was another step in the same vein. Knowing who he was, she could have taken him for an expensive dinner at a top class restaurant. He wouldn't have cared if she had, but he was delighted with her choice. It was in keeping with this whole encounter—totally off-the-wall.

"Titanic Thai, here I come!" he said out loud,

grinning to himself as he bounded up the stairs to the master bedroom of his Bondi Beach apartment. Shower, shave, change of clothes, get to Taylor Square, scout the restaurant…tonight he was going to get the princess with the magic rainbow smile and the heart of gold!

Erin knew that the most sensible course was to play it cool with Peter Ramsey, not look as if she expected anything from him, turn up in jeans and pretend she wasn't madly wishing he found her too desirable to pass up. Their lives were too different to envisage any serious relationship between them.

On the other hand, she'd never been so captivated by a man. Even if it could only be a mad fling with him…

Temptation wove its own more exciting path around common sense and was in full swing by the time she reached the Hyde Park apartment hotel where she invariably stayed while in Sydney. It was in easy walking distance of the Thai restaurant where she had frequently dined.

As she showered, washed and blow-dried her hair into a silky black mane that rippled over her shoulders, her mind moved into a totally reckless whirl of wanting to make something happen between her and Peter Ramsey. Her hands reached into the clothes cupboard and pulled out the lemon, lime and green dress. It was a gorgeous dress. She loved the colours and the colours loved her. It was also a wicked little dress. In fact, her London editor, Richard Long, who regularly tried to move their relationship into a sexual one, had described it as a bed-me dress.

It was halter-necked, virtually backless, had to be worn braless, the low V-neckline in front showing a seductive hint of cleavage. A wide tan leather belt drew attention to the curvy lines of her figure, and the soft fabric flowed into a frothy skirt that was deliciously feminine. Teamed with strappy tan leather sandals and no jewellery, it wasn't too, too dressy, Erin decided.

And so what if it did stir the pot tonight!

Peter Ramsey had appeared like magic in her life.

Why not use a bit of female witchery to keep him in it, at least for long enough to explore the feelings he'd aroused?

She was thirty years old and had virtually perfected the role of an onlooker of life, a passer-by who'd never felt truly wanted enough by anyone to become enmeshed in a deep involvement. A lasting attachment to Peter Ramsey was not really within the bounds of reason, but a brief one…a fiercely compelling conviction surged through her…that was worth going for, given that no other man had ever made such a deep impact on her.

* * *

Peter glanced at his watch as the waitress uncorked the bottle of chardonnay he'd bought from the liquor-mart next door and proceeded to pour him a glass of wine. Seven twenty-five. Only a few more minutes to wait if Erin was punctual. No reason for her not to be, he reasoned. Her choice of restaurant was very much a drop in place.

The front half of it was divided into a kitchen along one wall with a bench-seat along the wall facing it for takeaway customers to wait for their orders to be cooked. The back section had just two rows of five tables each side. He'd been led to the third one behind the kitchen, which provided privacy from the more transient customers.

The table had a laminated surface for easy cleaning. Paper serviettes were available from a dispenser. Pepper and salt and various sauces were contained in a holder. A corked bottle of water stood by two drinking glasses. If customers wanted to drink wine with their meal, it was a case of bring your own—information Peter had received when he'd arrived earlier. An ice bucket could be provided and was, the waitress leaving the bottle in it after she finished serving him.

He sipped the chardonnay—a fine Margaret River wine that he hoped would be to Erin's taste. He wanted to please her, wanted her to be pleased with him. This meeting place virtually shouted that to her mind, any romance between them was out of the question. No doubt, the Ramsey name had intimidated her into thinking that. A smile of happy anticipation spread across his face. He relished the challenge of overriding that barrier with a full-on charm offensive.

Except it wasn't needed.

That realisation hit him the moment Erin walked into his line of vision. There was nothing casual about her appearance. It was a full-on female offensive.

Desire to take what she was offering instantly kicked in. Erin Lavelle was an outstandingly gorgeous babe, long silky black hair swinging free, lush breasts free, too, playing peekaboo from a very sexy bodice. The dress she was wearing was a knockout—a stunning combination of colours that brought out the green in her eyes, and was styled to stir the juices of any red-blooded male.

Yes reverberated around in Peter's brain.

But it was tinged with disappointment—the challenge had just been snuffed out.

And laced with cynicism—was this a reaction to his name and all it stood for? Had rainbow girl decided to take a crack at the pot of gold?

Mistake!

Elation had bubbled through Erin as Peter Ramsey rose from the table to greet her, looking stunned by this more glamorous version of herself, but there was something wrong with his smile. It didn't reach his eyes. And it curled into a twist of irony.

Her fluttering heart closed its wings and shrunk inside itself. Her mind cringed with embarrassment. She'd misread his invitation to dinner. The attraction she felt towards him wasn't mutual and she'd just made a gigantic fool of herself.

Defence instincts sprang into action. The fertile creativity in her mind was fast-tracked into finding a scenario that would wipe out his impression of availability signals being flaunted.

"Hi!" she said brightly, quickening her step towards him, holding out her hand, fixing a wry little smile on her mouth. "Excuse the glad rags. A bit out of place here. But I'm going on to a party afterwards and it was easier not to have to do a change of clothes later."

"Please don't apologise. No man could look

at you tonight without feeling a sense of pleasure," he rolled out, politely intent on putting her at ease, though the hand holding hers made that impossible. It gripped hard, almost possessively, sending a charge of heat into her bloodstream. "Meeting up with your boyfriend?" he asked, a laser-intensity in the blue eyes scanning hers, jolting her into giving up the truth.

"I don't have a boyfriend."

An arched eyebrow expressed surprise. "Then I'm sure there'll be plenty of contenders for the position at the party."

She wasn't sure if that was a compliment or not, given the blatant sexiness of her dress. "But will I click with any of them?" she tossed out a touch ruefully, knowing how very rare that had been in her life, and the one possibility of it happening tonight was distancing himself from her.

"Very elusive, that click," he remarked dryly.

"You find that, too?" She was babbling—babbling because she was so knotted up inside, any words were better than silence.

"Why wouldn't I?"

The hard challenge in his eyes made her feel silly. It derided any assumption that everything was easy for him. She really had no idea what his life was like, had come to find out, but…this wasn't why he was here and she was putting every foot wrong.

"I'm sure you have a bigger choice of candidates for the click than I have," she shot out defensively.

"Believe me, that doesn't make it any less elusive."

"I'm told you've had a lot of women, Peter."

"Trial and error. How many errors have you made, Erin?"

She shook her head, completely rattled by the swift riposte and the highly personal probing in his eyes. "I'm sorry. I don't know how we moved onto this stuff. You wanted to know about Mrs Harper."

"And the errors made there," he agreed, releasing her hand and gesturing to the chair opposite his. "Are you in a hurry to get this dinner over with?"

The question flustered her. Everything about this meeting seemed to be going hopelessly awry, including her fiction about a party, which he naturally assumed would put a limit on this meeting. "No. No. Time doesn't matter," she muttered, settling on the chair and shooting him a look of appeal for a less pressured feeling to this meeting. "It's Thomas who matters. His life is being screwed up by warring parents."

"You care more about the child than the father?" Peter queried as he resumed his seat.

It made Erin pause to consider. "I guess I empathise more with Thomas. My own parents divorced when I was seven."

"Were you the only child?"

"Yes." She grimaced, remembering all too well the sense of being deserted. "A very lonely only child."

"Who got custody of you?"

"My mother."

"Was that what you wanted?"

"I wanted them to stay together." She flashed him a look of burning conviction. "You shouldn't have children if the marriage isn't rock solid."

"Is that why you haven't married? You've never felt secure enough in a relationship?"

This conversation was going right off the rails. She didn't want to analyse herself, not to him or anyone else. As it was, he'd drawn stuff from her she never talked about and it was none of his business. "We're not here to talk about me," she tersely reminded him.

"Just curious about where you're coming from," he said amiably, reaching for the bottle of wine, which was resting in an ice-bucket.

"This is a Margaret River Chardonnay. Would you like to share it with me?"

No way was she going to add alcohol to the volatile mix of feeling emotionally torn up by this man. Her tongue was running out of control and she needed to put a guard on it. She nodded to the corked bottle on the table. "I'll stick to water, thank you."

"Saving yourself for party drinks."

Erin paused to take stock of what was happening here. The party lie kept spawning questions that were pricking at her private life. Why was Peter Ramsey putting her so much on the spot if he had no personal interest in her?

His reaction to her attempt to look as attractive as she could had definitely been negative, yet since she'd dismissed her dressed up appearance as nothing to do with him, he seemed intent on finding out more about her than the main purpose of this meeting warranted.

Feeling uncomfortably confused with the situation, she looked him straight in the eye and belligerently stated, "No. I just prefer water. I like to keep a clear head."

"Even at a party?"

"Especially at a party."

"Had a bad experience," he assumed.

"No. And I don't want to invite one."

"Sounds like being in control is of prime importance to you."

He was boring in again, the piercing blue eyes focused so intensely on hers, answers to his questions had been spilling out as though drawn from her by a magnet. Despite being stone cold sober, Erin felt hopelessly out of control with Peter Ramsey. Her pulse was racing and her mind was struggling to keep up with his.

"I will not give control of my life to someone else," burst from her lips before she even realised how revealing that was about herself.

He zoomed straight in on it. "Being independent is safer than trusting anyone, Erin?"

"When the people you should be able to count on keep shuffling you around for their convenience, you learn independence pretty darned quick," she answered with considerable heat, feeling him burrowing under her skin, going deeper and deeper. "And that's probably what's in store for Thomas Harper," she added emphatically, trying to move this conversation onto the track it should be taking.

Needing action to break the highly charged current flowing between them, she turned and grabbed the bottle of water, proceeding to fill one of the glasses provided with a long, cool drink.

"I'm sorry. I should have done that for you."

The apology grated on her frayed nerves. "Why?" she shot at him.

He shrugged, his mouth twitching into a

bemused little smile. "It's what a gentleman does for a lady."

"And what does a lady do for a gentleman in your world, Peter?"

She goes to bed with him.

The cynical thought was in her mind, even as she posed the question. Nevertheless, it came as a shock when she read it in his eyes, the sudden simmer of desire directed straight at her.

Even his smile seemed sensually seductive as he answered, "In my world a gentleman looks after a lady who answers his needs."

Her mind was in an absolute whirl. "What need am I answering?" shot straight out of her mouth.

"My need to talk with you."

His reply was so smooth, his expression shifting so swiftly to serious sincerity, Erin wondered if she'd imagined the hot flash of desire. But her skin was still tingling from it.

Fortunately the waitress arrived at their table to take their meal orders, diverting Peter

Ramsey's attention and giving Erin a breathing space. She needed a blast of oxygen in her brain to clear her confusion and get some reasonable perspective on what had eventuated from this meeting so far.

She had paraded her wish to be desirable to him with blatant honesty.

He hadn't liked it.

Yet now…did he find a hard-to-get scenario more stimulating—the challenge of winning over resistance? Perhaps he'd had too many women offering themselves to him on a platter and he'd envisaged her being different—more of a novelty for him, like her choice of this restaurant.

She sighed.

Nothing in real life was simple.

Which was why she much preferred living in the stories she made up in her mind. She had total control over how her characters acted and what their response to each other would be.

"Erin?"

Peter's prompt snapped her out of fantasy and back to the immediate demands of the present. She smiled at the waitress. "I'll have the Chilli Jam Prawns."

"You like hot?" Peter queried.

"Chilli Jam is more spicy than hot," Erin informed him.

"I'll have the same," he instructed the waitress who ticked off the order and departed to take it to the kitchen.

Peter flashed a devil-may-care grin at Erin. "I like spicy."

Her stomach cramped, battling the butterflies that were suddenly swarming through it. That grin…the wickedly sexy sparkle in his eyes… he was applying *spicy* to her…had to be… yet…

She cocked her head, looking askance at him, trying to be more objective—sensible— about what Peter Ramsey was doing here.

"Why do I get the feeling you're being adventurous tonight?"

He laughed and Erin felt the sheer joy of the sound rippling through her, stroking chords of pleasure that totally erased the dark swirl of confusion and left her earlier feelings about this man bubbling brightly in her mind.

He shone above every other man she'd met.

She wanted to experience everything about him.

So her best course was to try to relax and roll with whatever he wanted to say and do, see where it led.

CHAPTER FOUR

SHE had that look of curious wonder in her lovely green eyes again—almost childlike in its wishful search for understanding.

It tugged at Peter. He barely resisted the urge to tell her, "You're my adventure, Erin Lavelle."

That truth could very well offend her, make her withdraw from him, halt his progress in finding out more about her. So far, it was all good. No boyfriend. What family she had—divorced parents—had no strong claim on her. She was free to do whatever she chose, and tonight she'd chosen to have dinner with him before going off to a party.

Not that she would get to that party.

Peter was determined on holding her with him.

"Today has not been my usual scene," he conceded, aware she wanted to be given a reasonable explanation for his actions. "But it has felt surprisingly good and I guess I want to finish it up still feeling good."

"Why were you in the park?" she asked, pinning him down to detail.

Because you were there.

Would she be flattered to hear that?

Or frightened?

His hunting instincts warned it was better to get closer to her before showing his hand. He shrugged and answered, "The whim of a moment. I'd spent the morning at Randwick Racecourse, meeting with my trainer. The Autumn Racing Carnival is coming up and he wanted to discuss the form of the horses I own. I was driving back into the city, thinking what a beautiful day it was." His smile invited her to smile back at him as he added, "The urge to stop and smell the roses came upon me."

She laughed at his whimsy. "There are no roses in that park."

"Fresh air then," he supplanted. "You don't get fresh air and sunshine in boardrooms."

Her eyes danced with amusement. "When was the last time you played hookey from your usual life?"

He shook his head. "I can't remember."

"And it still feels good—" she gestured to their downmarket surroundings "—being here?"

His eyes lightly teased as he answered, "How could it not when a princess sweeps in, wanting to bring joy to a child for evermore?"

"Oh!" Her hands flew up to cup cheeks that suddenly bloomed rose-red. "You really were listening to me tell that story!"

"You had those children—and me—totally rapt."

"You liked it?" She glowed with delight, as

though such an accolade was totally unexpected and an immense pleasure.

"You have a very special gift, Erin," he
assured her.

"That's one of my favourite stories. I'm so
glad it…" She stopped, frowned as though
having second thoughts about the rush of uninhibited enthusiasm. Her lashes lowered and
he caught the sense that she was hiding something from him.

"Go on," he urged, wanting the happy animation on her face to return. It was so open and
unaffected.

She flashed him a self-deprecating little smile
and picked up her glass of water. "I was getting
carried away by your compliment, Peter. And
I do thank you for it, but let's talk about the
Harper family now. That *is* what you came for."

It was on the tip of his tongue to deny it. He
had come for her. He could have asked for and
received a report on Dave's ex-wife over the

telephone. But it was probably too soon for Erin to feel comfortable about being the sole focus of his attention. Better to get the Harper family issue out of the way first.

Adopting an expression of eager interest, he opened up with, "I presume your aunt used my business card and explained my intervention on Dave's behalf?"

"Not to begin with. She told Mrs Harper about Thomas's father turning up in the park and…" Erin frowned over the recollection. "It was weird, Peter. Instead of being angry or frightened or agitated…she looked triumphant as though he'd walked into a trap she'd set for him. Her body language was all hyped up eagerness as she asked if the police had been called to take him away."

Peter nodded. "That fits with Dave's story. She wants Thomas to herself with Dave right out of both their lives, and she's pursuing every nasty ruse to bring about that outcome. I imagine your aunt was subjected to a blast of angry frustration when the answer was negative."

"It was like a bomb going off." The shock of it widened her eyes and coloured her voice as she described the reaction. "Abuse, threats, insults. Mrs Harper's face was red with fury by the time Sarah managed to cut through the tantrum, handing her your business card and relaying your support for Mr Harper."

"What happened then?"

"Well, your name certainly knocked the stuffing out of her. She didn't want to believe it. Kept saying things like… How could Dave know him? Why would he stick his oar in? It's got nothing to do with him. Anyhow, Sarah told her you were very definitely taking an interest on Mr Harper's behalf. Then she got hysterical, almost screaming that it was her life and she was going to live it her way."

"That fits, too," Peter said, satisfied he was supporting a just case. "Dave said he always had to give in to her for the sake of peace, but he couldn't bear having his son taken from him."

"I think she'll fight it right down to the wire," Erin warned, "I think she's too used to getting her own way not to."

"I don't doubt that. But I've put Dave in the hands of a lawyer who will ensure appropriate visiting rights and take the custody battle to court. It won't go all her way."

His confidence clearly piqued her interest. "Why have you involved yourself, Peter? I mean... Mrs Harper had a point. Why stick your oar in when it's none of your business?"

"Do you disapprove?"

"No. Not at all. It's just...well...just not what people generally do, taking a stranger on board and doing what you can for him."

She was impressed and intrigued by his generosity. Peter knew he could capitalise on her admiration but he never felt comfortable when money was behind it. "When you have

all the advantages of great wealth at your fin-
gertips, it's easy to play The Good Samaritan,
Erin," he said sardonically.

"I guess that's true," she said slowly, thought-
fully. "But this wasn't just tossing money at
him. You gave him your time, as well. Went out
of your way to fix things for him."

"I didn't want him to lose his son. It's not
right what happens with divorce. Too many
fathers are cast adrift without their family. I
know if it happened to me I'd fight tooth and
nail for my children."

Erin believed him. The hard, ruthless edge in
his voice, the brooding expression on his face,
the glint of hell-bent determination in his
eyes—the thought ran through her mind and
shivered down her spine—heaven help the
woman who tried to separate Peter Ramsey
from his children! The Viking warrior would
go into battle with a vengeance.

But would it be from a sense of possession or did he really intend to be a hands-on parent?

"Not all fathers want the responsibility of raising their children," she said quietly. "They prefer to leave it to the mothers."

A flash of hard mockery preceded a swift switch to the laser probing. "Is that your personal experience, Erin?"

"Yes, it is," she conceded, adding her own touch of mockery as she explained. "My father is an academic, a professor of English, who lives in the rarefied world of literature. He takes it for granted that his needs will be looked after by a woman. A child's needs…" She shook her head, smiling wryly. "He only ever did what suited him and that was mainly talking books to me. Which I liked. But I was always aware that our relationship was limited to what he enjoyed doing. I didn't really exist for him beyond that bit of sharing. In fact, I rather painfully learnt…after my parents separated...there was no point in asking him for more."

Peter grimaced. "A totally self-centred man. I'm sorry, Erin. We're not all like that."

"No. And all women aren't like Mrs Harper."

"Your mother didn't want you, either?"

Erin hesitated. Her comment on Thomas's mother had been aimed at what she sensed was a general cynicism about women, wanting him to review his attitude. Another probe into what was deeply personal to her made her feel uncomfortably vulnerable. She'd just revealed more to Peter Ramsey about her childhood than she'd ever revealed to anyone. Somehow the issue with the Harper family had lured her into it...or was it the keen interest in the riveting blue eyes?

Did it matter if she told him how it had been for her? They were simply talking around the consequences of divorce. This was a one-off night in their lives so it was highly unlikely that any private information she gave him would come back to bite her in a discomfiting fashion. Besides, answering his questions gave her grounds for demanding he answer hers.

"I wouldn't go so far as to say my mother didn't want me, but she bitterly resented my father not doing his share, so she kept pushing me at him. In hindsight, I realise she hated having been displaced by another woman and used me to spike his new comfort zone as much as she could."

"So your father left her."

Erin sighed, remembering all the yelling and screaming that had preceded the separation, shutting herself in her bedroom, trying not to hear, desperately wishing it would stop. "My mother discovered he was having an affair and made it impossible for him to stay," she said flatly.

"Sounds like she cared more about making him pay for his infidelity than she cared about you, Erin. Is that how it was?" Peter asked sympathetically.

She shrugged, her mind instinctively sheering away from the lonely steps of learning how to cope by herself, preferring not to ask anything of her parents than suffer more rejection from her father or a harangue from her mother about how difficult it was, being a single parent.

"I guess I learnt to detach myself from both of them. I think a lot of children become victims of the emotional crossfire that divorce invariably triggers." She heaved another sigh, which drifted into an appreciative smile for his concern. "I hope Thomas gets to feel good with his father. And I hope his mother comes around to understanding that he needs both parents to love him."

"I hope so, too."

"So what about you, Peter?"

The question caught him by surprise. She

could see he was still sifting through her personal experience of divorce, perhaps applying it to his Good Samaritan act and wondering if it would lead to a better life for Thomas Harper. He looked quizzically at her as he repeated, "What about me?"

"What's it like to have been born and raised as a prince, able to distribute largesse on a whim?"

She had tossed the question at him lightly but his face hardened as though she'd hit a raw nerve. "Does anyone really care about a prince as a person, or do they simply work at getting close and staying close for what he can do for them? What they can get out of him? The largesse they might be able to tap?" One eyebrow lifted in sardonic challenge. "You'd be surprised how lonely that life can be, Erin."

She stared at him, wondering if his trust in friendship had been totally tainted by the wealth at his disposal. It was a sad situation if that was his reality. She could see why he'd feel good about giving to Dave Harper because it hadn't been expected of him, hadn't been asked for.

Their meals arrived. Once their plates were set in front of them and the waitress gone, Erin leaned forward to say, "I'll be paying for my dinner, Peter. I didn't come for a free ride."

She'd come for something else entirely—an adventure with him.

"I did ask you to join me, Erin," he pointed out, amused by her independent stance.

"My choice," she reminded him. "Let's eat."

The food was good; fresh vegetables lightly cooked, succulent king prawns, flavours enhanced by the spicy chilli jam. "Enjoying it?" she asked, hoping that her choice was to his liking.

"Mmm…very tasty."

His eyes locked with hers for a moment, a bombardment of bright blue twinkles arousing the strong sensation he was once again applying the words to her, not the meal. She kept eating but the excitement racing around her mind made the action completely mechanical.

"Sure you wouldn't like a glass of wine?" he asked, lifting the bottle from the ice-bucket.

Erin shook her head, feeling she was intoxicated enough just being with him. When he replaced the bottle without refilling his glass, she said, "Please don't let me stop you from enjoying it."

"I have to keep a clear head, too. I'm driving."

Away from this meeting place.

The thought delivered a shaft of cold sanity. Erin once more berated herself for being so foolish as to think he might want to extend this connection with her. Hadn't he just more or less rebuffed her attempt to delve into his life? He was now assured he'd done the right thing by Dave and Thomas Harper. Once this dinner was over...and it was...both of them setting their emptied plates aside for the waitress to collect…there was no reason for him to prolong this encounter.

Unless…

She couldn't suppress the hope for something more.

"Do you have far to drive?" she asked, trying to force herself to accept the inevitable.

"No. It's only a short distance to Bondi Beach."

"Is that where you live?"

"I have an apartment there." His mouth curved into a dry little smile. "I live in many places, Erin."

"So do I," tripped off her tongue.

It caused him to look at her quizzically.

She didn't want to talk about herself anymore, didn't want him to stay on out of politeness, listening to the kind of footloose life she had adopted. Besides, most people considered her odd—those who had roots they cared about. Rather than be seen as odd by this man, she laughed and said, "I can go anywhere in my mind, Peter."

He smiled his understanding. "You must have a vivid imagination to tell stories so well. Can your mind encompass going with me tonight?"

The question was slid out so smoothly, tapping straight into her own secret desire, Erin wasn't sure if it had really been spoken. "I beg your pardon?" she rattled out, her heart thumping so hard her chest hurt.

He leaned forward, bringing the full power of his physical magnetism into play as he spread his hands out to her in open appeal across the table. His eyes engaged hers with almost hypnotic intensity as he said, "You're not committed to meeting anyone in particular at your party."

"No." There was no party.

"So come with me instead." His mouth broke into a dazzling white grin. "Think about it. It's only right for the prince to sweep Cinderella off to his castle. We can't let the story end here, Erin."

Her mouth had gone completely dry. She swallowed hard to work some moisture into it as her dazed mind came to grips with a move she'd given up believing would happen. Peter Ramsey *was* attracted to her. He wanted her to go with him, be with him.

"No. Ending it here wouldn't feel good," she blurted out, throwing all sense of caution to the wind.

He laughed, delighted with her reply. "Click!" he said, reminding her of their earlier conversation about finding someone who was tuned in on the same wavelength. "My horse awaits," he added, rising to his feet and holding out his hand to draw her to hers.

"Is it a white charger?" she asked giddily, her hand shooting up to meet his, her body lifting from the chair in a surge of wild happiness.

"Blue," he replied with mock ruefulness. "But it is charged with a lot of horsepower."

She laughed, deliriously aware of his fingers enclosing hers, forging a link that was not about to let her slip away from him. A brief separation came as they paused on their way out of the restaurant to pay for the dinner, but once that was done, Peter instantly recaptured her hand and maintained the connection while they walked along together.

It was Friday night and Oxford Street was thronged with people intent on having a good time at the end of their working week. Despite the boisterous crowd milling around them, they moved in a space of their own, as though the big man beside her generated a force-field that kept others from touching them. They occupied a magic circle, Erin thought fancifully, refusing to think about where they were going, revelling in the exhilarating sense of not knowing what might come next.

They turned a corner. "Parking stable in the next block," Peter informed her, still enjoying the fiction she had fallen in with.

Her feet wanted to dance. She did feel like Cinderella, miraculously going to the prince's ball. "I wonder if we can stop the clock from striking twelve," she said whimsically.

"Are you planning on running away at midnight?"

"That's when this day ends," she reminded him, secretly hoping that the adventure they were embarking upon would keep its exciting fascination for both of them.

"I do have a glass slipper up my sleeve," he said with arch confidence.

"You do?"

He grinned. "I know where you work so I can find you again."

She didn't work at the preschool, but he could find her through her aunt if he really wanted to. A fountain of joy was bubbling through her as they entered the parking station. She felt no trepidation whatsoever about accompanying him anywhere at all. It seemed to her that a fairy godmother had waved her wand, ordaining their coming together, because however unlikely it was, they were meant to meet.

This lovely sense of a benign Fate was abruptly shaken when Peter led her to a royal-blue BMW Z4 sports convertible. It was too coincidental for her to be personally confronted by two such cars on the same day. Her heart quivered with shock as her mind made the obvious connection. She turned to Peter, her eyes searching for the truth in his.

"It was you at the pedestrian crossing near the preschool."

"Yes, it was," he acknowledged without the slightest hesitation.

"And then…then you just happened to drop in at that park?"

"No. Your smile drew me there."

"My smile…"

Bright red danger flashes were popping in her mind. This was crazy. A man as powerful as Peter Ramsey stopping for a woman he thought was a preschool teacher? It was too far out…too…

His hand was suddenly cupping her cheek, its warmth arousing an instant pleasure in his touch. She automatically leaned into it. His fingers gently stroked her temple, somehow soothing the tumult his words had triggered. *He* smiled, making it seem perfectly reasonable that a smile could have immense drawing power. Her throat had seized up. She was speechless, staring at the unmistakable glitter of desire in his eyes—desire for her, no longer hidden—desire intent on being satisfied.

His head was bending down, coming closer.

He was going to kiss her.

A moment before his lips touched hers, one

last panicky thought broke through the mesmerised state of acceptance—what kind of man would do all Peter Ramsey had done to get to this moment with her...*just from seeing her in the street?*

CHAPTER FIVE

ERIN'S heart was galloping. The light brush of his lips against hers caused an electric buzz. She ceased to think. The tip of her tongue darted out to sweep over the acute sensation. He sucked it into his mouth, instantly turning the kiss into a deeply intimate connection.

She felt him lift her hand to his shoulder, felt the fingers that had been stroking her face slide into her hair, felt his arm slide around her waist. Then her body was being pressed against his and it felt so good to be held there, her soft femininity revelling in his hard strength, her breasts swelling ecstatically across the hot, muscular wall of his chest, a wild excitement coursing through her stomach at the unmistakable evidence of his desire, her thighs quivering at the tension in his, the sense of melting into him spreading right through her as the kiss went on and on, erotically gathering an urgent passion that was totally beyond any experience she'd ever had of kissing.

She wasn't aware of thrusting her own hand into his hair, holding his head down to hers, wasn't aware that her other hand was clamped to his back, doing its utmost to increase the pressure of their embrace. Only when Peter's mouth broke from hers did she become conscious of her own lustful complicity in what he had started.

"I want you very badly, Erin Lavelle." Words bursting through ragged breathing.

"Yes," fell from her lips before she gathered wits enough to know what she was saying.

"Into the car," came the gruff command.

Erin felt like a bundle of jelly. Peter virtually

scooped her into the passenger seat of the BMW, deftly fastening her seat belt before closing her door and striding around the bonnet to the driver's side. She dazedly wondered how he could summon so much forceful purpose when her body seemed to have lost all sense of co-ordination.

He whooshed into the seat beside her, charging the air inside the car with his highly active energy. The powerful engine of the sports convertible thrummed into life. He flashed a grin at her. "Will you be worried about your hair getting blown about if I put the hood down?"

"No," she said, thinking a cooling breeze might help glue her back together.

Peter pressed a button and the hood lifted up and disappeared behind them. Then they were off, heading out of the parking station, driving into the night. Red traffic lights stopped them at the Oxford Street intersection. Pedestrians streamed across the road in front of them. People looked at the car, just as she had earlier today, looked at the occupants to check what they were like.

Was Peter eyeing the women as they passed? She glanced sharply at him.

He wasn't smiling at any of them. His attention was trained on the traffic lights, waiting for them to turn green. Impatient to get where they were going? He either caught her glance out of the corner of his eye or sensed her unease.

"What?" he asked, his gaze spearing to hers, the blue eyes alert to a possible problem.

The sense of taking a huge risk with him made her blurt out, "Is it a game with you, picking out a woman who's outside your social circle and—"

"No," he broke in emphatically. His hand moved swiftly from the gear stick, reaching for one of hers and giving it a reassuring squeeze. "You're a first, Erin. And you shine more brightly than any woman who's ever been in my social circle. My life has seemed grey for a long time and today you put colour into it."

A first…

She liked that.

It made her feel special.

She smiled.

He smiled back.

Warmth curled around her heart and calmed the spurt of agitation in her mind.

The lights turned green. Peter released her hand and drove on. Erin relaxed into the contoured leather seat, telling herself to enjoy the ride in a sports convertible, the sense of being open to the night, air rushing past, ruffling her hair, the sights and scents of the city much sharper than from a closed car.

She wanted to be simply swept along by this man, let whatever happened with him happen, even if it was madly reckless. Yet a natural wariness in her mind kept pricking at a hardy strain of common sense. He might have lied about her being the first. He might get his kicks from taking a trip with a woman he chose out of nowhere.

He had definitely manipulated the situation today, directing her personal co-operation with his plan to defuse the traumatic scene with Dave Harper, appointing her as the person to collect Thomas from his father, giving her his business card and pressing her to contact him, motivating her to meet him again. None of it was really spontaneous. All of it spoke of a man primed to seize opportunity and turn it to his advantage.

Peter Ramsey…billionaire…ruthless in going after what he wanted and getting it?

Here she was, taking a ride straight to his bedroom, right where he wanted her, maybe where he'd decided he'd like to have her from the moment she'd smiled at him. A Latin phrase her father was fond of quoting slid into her mind, Julius Caesar's famous boast…*Veni, vidi, vici*…I came, I saw, I conquered.

In a way, billionaires were the modern day version of empire-builders, taking over whatever piece of the world fired their interest. There was no doubt in her mind now that Peter Ramsey was of that special breed of men. Hadn't she instinctively picked that up, casting him as a Viking warrior even before she'd known who he was?

Maybe she should be frightened of him but she wasn't. He excited her, more than any man she had ever met. So what if she had been his puppet today, being pulled by strings she hadn't seen! She still wanted this adventure with him, and had tried to pull strings herself to get it, deliberately sexing up her appearance. Her life had been grey for a long time, which was why she immersed herself so much in her stories. She'd used them to colour it. And her travels through other countries…looking for colour, wanting it.

Click!

She and Peter Ramsey were together on that tonight.

Her prince...his princess...more than likely a one-night fantasy, but let it be, she thought fiercely.

Let it be.

Peter had to keep cautioning himself not to exceed the speed limit as he drove. Exhilaration was pumping through him and it craved action. Fast action. He was acutely conscious of Erin's presence beside him, could still feel the imprint of her body on his...so soft and giving, stirring caveman instincts that were running rampant.

He was so caught up in his own physical excitement, it was a while before he realised she'd said nothing since the Oxford Street intersection. Most women were full of chatter. He didn't want to talk, didn't want to break the sense of being drawn into a magical tunnel that promised the fulfilment of all he wanted with a woman. Fantasy, perhaps, but the urge to give it free rein tonight was galloping through him.

Yet was her silence one of contented acquiescence to spending this night with him, or did it hide less harmonious thoughts?

She'd said yes.

But then there'd been the question about his motives for pursuing a connection with her— *a game he played.* Had she been satisfied with his reply? How was she to know he'd never done this before?

He shot a quick assessing glance at her. Her head was tilted back against the headrest, eyes closed, long strands of hair blowing into a feathering dance around her face. No troubled frown. No sign of tension. Her expression was completely serene, her body relaxed, her hands loosely linked in her lap.

Was she, too, floating with the night, not letting any worry touch it?

Recalling a comment she'd made over dinner, he quietly asked, "Where have you gone in your mind, Erin?"

"I'm right here, living this moment with you," she answered and he could hear the smile in her voice.

"It feels good?" he prompted, wanting confirmation.

"It feels…marvellous."

The eloquent thrill in her voice relieved him of any concern about how she was reacting to his initiatives in getting to this moment.

She was with him.

Or was she with the Ramsey billions, dismissing any sense of risk in favour of riding this opportunity to get into a relationship with him and…

His jaw clenched in frustration. He didn't want to think like that with Erin. Not tonight.

Just go with the flow. Don't spoil it, he told himself savagely. She was beautiful, delightful, and cynical thoughts would blunt his desire for her and tarnish the magic. Block them out, let them go, enjoy having this woman.

His castle was a penthouse apartment, set up on the hill overlooking Bondi Beach. An elevator from the basement garage took them straight to a spacious living room, which spread out to a terrace with a swimming pool. Erin caught only a glimpse of these luxurious surroundings in passing. Peter led her straight up a staircase which took them to the master bedroom where he opened a wall of curtains, revealing a view that instantly evoked the sense of being on top of the world.

There was a balcony outside. He slid glass doors apart, smiled and ushered her to the railing, staying behind her, his arms encircling her waist, his head bent close to hers, his breath warming her ear as he murmured, "This night is ours, Erin."

"Yes," she whispered, a huge welling of emotion sighing through her voice. It was a beautiful cloudless night, stars twinkling above the far horizon, a crescent moon shining brightly, a light breeze wafting the salty scent of the sea, the rhythmic roar of waves rushing onto the beach and withdrawing. But what made it incredibly special was the presence of the man who was holding her.

She leaned back against him, nestling her head into the curve of his neck and shoulder, loving his strong masculinity, feeling safe in his embrace, safer than she had ever felt in her life. Which was strange because she barely knew Peter Ramsey, yet her instincts said *trust him.* He was a big man, big in every way, a man who would fight for what he believed was right, a man who would protect what he held dear to the last breath in his body.

"You feel so good," he said as though bemused by his own feelings with her.

"You do, too," she answered, unhesitant about stating what was true for her.

"I want to feel all of you, Erin." His hands moved to the buckle of her belt. "Mind if I undress you out here?"

"No, I don't mind." She wanted to feel his hands on her, all over her. Her mind was sure his touch would be magic, but her body wanted him to be naked, too, naked to the night in a dark, primitive world of absolute togetherness. "As long as you don't mind me taking your clothes off, as well."

He laughed, a deep throaty sound of pleasure that made her pulse race with excitement. She'd had sex many times before; out of curiosity, out of loneliness, out of a need to hold onto a relationship, hoping that the physical intimacy would forge a deeper bond, though it never had. Too much else always got in the way—degrees of separation becoming bigger and bigger, leaving her alone again.

Tonight was different. Her whole being was bubbling with anticipation. There was no history of before, no expectation of after. The only reality was here and now and she'd never felt so brilliantly alive.

He undid her belt, slid it away from her waist. She heard the buckle clank onto the tiled floor of the balcony. He ran featherlight fingers up her arms, over her shoulders, raising a host of goose-bumps on her skin.

"Cold?" he asked, parting the long tresses of her hair to bare the halter neck-strap.

"No. I think madly stimulated covers it."

He laughed again—happy laughter that made her heart dance with exhilaration. "Same for me," he said, kissing her nape as he separated the straps that had held her bodice in place.

Her scalp tingled. The heat from his mouth burned a trail right from her head to her toes.

The top of her dress slid down, leaving her breasts naked to the cooling breeze from the sea. Her nipples tightened into longer, harder protrusions, sensitive to the sudden freedom and change of temperature. Then the zipper at the back of her waist was released and her skirt slithered down to her feet. Thumbs hooked into the G-string, which was the only other garment she wore. It was lowered in a quick swoop.

"Lift your feet, one at a time, Erin."

She did as she was told, listening to the rustle of her clothes being swept out of the way. He did not remove her sandals. It was unbelievably erotic, standing in strappy high-heels while his fingers circled her fine-boned ankles, then drifted upwards, caressing her calves, gently rubbing the hollow behind her knees, stroking her thighs, hands cupping and gently squeezing the soft roundness of her buttocks, then gliding around the curve of her hips to spread across her stomach, fingers fanning back and forth over the sensitive area beneath her hip-bones.

Her heart was not dancing anymore. It was a wildly thumping drum. Her mind was so tightly focussed on his touch, she barely re-membered to breathe, only releasing and scooping in air when her chest threatened to burst. Every muscle in her body was quivering from a sensory overload. Her breasts seemed to be swelling, yearning for his hands to be on them. Then they were, possessively encasing them, the hard nipples trapped between fingers that used a rolling friction to excite them into even more prominence.

The desire to feel him in the same way surged over her enthralment with his touch. She grasped his hands and pulled them down, took a deep breath to fire herself up for action and swivelled around to face him.

"You, now," she said insistently.

He looked startled, frowning slightly, maybe

not liking the abrupt interruption to his taking pleasure in *her* body. Erin's stomach contracted in nervous apprehension. Had she broken the magic spell of the night? Spoiled what could have been?

Relief poured through her as his expression cleared, his eyes lighting with amused understanding, a wide grin assuring her of acceptance. "Control is yours, Erin. Do what you want with it."

Control?

The realisation flashed through her mind that he was remembering what she'd said over dinner… *I will not give control of my life to someone else.* But she had tonight, letting him take over, submitting to his lead, *trusting* him…

Why?

Because it felt right to be with him.

And he was proving it was right by putting himself in her hands. He might stride across his own world with all the self-assurance of a giant, but he was also a giver, and big enough for his male ego not to be threatened by anything she did. He was saying, *go for it.*

An exultant joy raced through Erin. He was giving her complete freedom to do whatever she wanted with him. "Okay…" A heady sense of power beamed through her grin back at him. "Your princess commands you not to move unless she says so."

He laughed—sparkling delight in her picking up the fantasy he had initiated.

"You are to watch the night while you feel my touch," she went on, wanting him to experience the same sensory pleasure he had given her.

"I shall pretend I'm on guard duty," he said, lifting his head to gaze steadily out to sea, a smile still quirking the corners of his mouth.

"Yes. Like the Beefeaters at Buckingham Palace."

"Have you been to Buckingham Palace?"

"You mustn't talk, Peter. Just focus on feeling."

She started unbuttoning his shirt, lightly running her fingernails down the gap of bared skin from button to button. He remained silent, except for the slight hissing sound of quickly sucked in breath. She smiled, knowing he was excited, and probably buzzing with anticipation of her next move.

Being passive could not be natural to a man like him, but it did force his mind off action and onto response, which would surely heighten every sensation she stirred with her touch. She wanted this night to be as different for him as it was for her—a wonderful memory to be cherished in the secret archives of their minds, something separate from their real lives but so intensely real it would never be forgotten.

The shirt slid easily off his shoulders and down his arms—such broad shoulders and powerfully muscled arms. And his chest was magnificently male. Satin-smooth, taut skin— marvellous to touch, feeling the strength of the man pulsing underneath it. Her hands glided over its living warmth, glorying in the freedom to roam over his splendid body. Her fingers tugged teasingly on his nipples, drawing them into hard nubs. The impulse to kiss them, suck on them, drove her straight into doing it.

She heard him growl and his hands were suddenly raking through her hair, holding her fiercely to him. A wild elation at his need for her burst through her mind, but she broke his grip, wanting to carry through what she'd set out to do.

"You're breaking the rules, Peter," she cried.

"Erin…" It was a groan of protest.

"I haven't fully undressed you," she pleaded.

His chest heaved as he regathered himself, his hands falling back to his sides, his body stiffening with resolve.

"It will be good," she promised huskily.

* * *

Good…

The word bounced around the fragmented edges of Peter's completely blown mind, not finding any relevant echo to what he was feeling. His entire body was a furnace of desire. Never had he been so aroused by a woman's touch. In fact, no woman had ever touched him with such exquisite sensuality. The intensity of feeling was such that he wanted to crush her flesh to his. Waiting was hell, yet there was a compelling fascination in what she would choose to do next.

It took every ounce of his control to hold still as she undid his jeans, slid her hands under the waistband of his underpants and slowly peeled both garments down, freeing his erection, causing the muscles in his butt to clench. Normally he shoved these clothes off as fast as possible. It was strange having them removed almost ceremoniously, standing here in the night air, having his body gradually bared; thighs, knees, calves, feet.

Were the princes of old ministered to like this by their valets?

The whimsical thought amused him until the answer took his breath away. No. Not like this. Not with soft hands stroking his legs, exploring every inch of them, making his skin leap with sensitivity, his muscles rock-hard. The roar of the ocean filled his ears. Or was it the roar of his own blood, rushing through his body?

She was circling his groin now, fingers playing with his pubic hair. He stared at the stars in the night sky, trying to repress the urge to explode into action. She was building a level of excitement that went beyond his experience and he wanted to know how far it could go. Would go. He had to hold himself in check, let the erotic assault continue.

A crescent moon…should be a full one for this fantasy. Though what he was feeling was no fantasy. She slid a hand between his thighs, cupping him, fingers gently squeezing, other fingers stroking the length of his shaft, gliding over its tip. She kissed it. He closed his eyes as a tide of incredibly sweet pleasure swamped his entire body.

She kissed his navel, kisses running up his chest as she pushed herself upright, her breasts brushing over him, her stomach pressing against his erection, her hands gliding up over his shoulders, linking behind his neck.

"Was it good?" she asked, her voice lilting with her own pleasure in him.

His eyes snapped open. Her face was lifted to his, her beautiful smile tugging on his heart again, releasing him from her rules of play. "This is not the end," he said, his hands whipping out to seize her, crush her close, his mouth crashing down on her smile, plundering it for all she would give him.

A fierce passion surged between them.

Man-woman heat sizzling, blazing.

Peter erupted into action, sweeping her off

her feet, cradling her in his arms, carrying her inside to his cave…his bed.

It was a long way from the end.

CHAPTER SIX

ERIN drifted slowly from a lovely languorous sleep, a deep sense of well-being seeping into her consciousness, her body uncurling and stretching, revelling in feeling good. She lifted her arms up over her head, arched her back and opened her eyes.

Shock slammed into her heart.

Peter Ramsey was standing at the end of the bed, watching her, a satisfied little smile lurking on his lips, his hair wet, slicked back, his blue eyes taking their fill of her, his magnificent body unashamedly naked except for a white towel slung over one shoulder.

He was definitely real.

And she was in his bed, his apartment at Bondi Beach.

Memories of all they'd done together last night flooded through Erin's mind. Her vaginal muscles instantly squinched, recalling the incredible pleasure of one amazing climax after another. It had been so fantastic, but...*what happens now?*

"Sleeping beauty awakes," Peter drawled in an indulgent tone. "You could have waited for my kiss."

Relief poured into her smile. He wasn't setting their fantasy aside yet. Maybe there would be more than one night. Lots of nights. "I haven't slept for a hundred years, have I?" she tossed back at him, wondering what time it was and if he had any plans for today—plans that included her.

"No. But it's time you were up if you want to come to the races with me."

"Races?"

"I have a horse running at Randwick this afternoon. It's her maiden race and I said I'd be there to watch."

Horse-racing! Erin recollected he'd met with his trainer yesterday morning. Billionaire playground, she thought. It had never been a part of her world but she was up for any new experience shared with this man. More adventure. Colourful, too.

"Do people dress up for Randwick as much as they do for the Melbourne Cup?" she asked, having watched what was always billed as "The Race That Stops A Nation" on television. It was a huge fashion scene.

"Don't worry about that," he said, arrogantly dismissive of the clothes aspect, strolling around the bed to sit beside her, smiling as he stroked the mussed tresses of her hair away from her face. "I'll dress you like a princess."

The connection to their fantasy didn't work for Erin this time. It was okay for Peter to invite her to go along with him. She wanted to. But dressing her…did he mean what she thought he meant?

"How do you intend to do that?" she asked warily.

He shrugged. "I'm acquainted with the top designers in Sydney. All it takes is a call to get something suitable brought here. What style of clothes appeals to you… Lisa Ho, Peter Morrisey, Colette Dinnegan…?"

He hung the celebrity names out with such a blasé air of confidence, Erin felt herself bridling against his assumption that she would fall in with his plan—be his mannequin—because he had the power and the wealth to dress her any way he pleased.

"No, thank you," she said decisively.

"No?" The caressing hand stilled. He frowned in disbelief. "You're saying no?"

His eyes blazed into hers, determined on re-igniting the intimate connection they had made last night. It had been good…great…incredibly fantastic…and her body instantly rebelled against any negative dictate that might end it right here. She wanted to be with him, wanted what they'd shared to continue, yet some gritty part of her brain would not let her be taken over or made over by anyone. If Peter thought he could buy her compliance…where was any respect for her in that?

"You don't own me, Peter," she said quietly. "Last night I chose to be with you and I still have the right to choose what works for me."

His frown deepened. "You can't want to end it now."

They were fighting words. He was gearing up to battle any barrier she threw at him. Which was certainly proof that he cared about keeping her, though whether that was for the sex or driven by an attraction on a deeper level, Erin couldn't tell.

The tension emanating from him tore along

her own nerves. She didn't want to be in conflict with this man. He was special. Uniquely special. But this was real life now, not an impulsive adventure, and real life had taught her that any kind of domination was bad.

She'd had too many experiences with men who expected her to fall into line with them, following wherever they led, not even con-sidering or respecting the fact that she had a mind of her own—a mind that would not play second fiddle to anyone else's. As powerful as Peter Ramsey undoubtedly was, Erin was not about to crumble under his will.

"I'd be happy to accompany you to the races, but not as your doll," she said determinedly.

"Doll?"

He didn't like the description, but Erin couldn't think of anything more apt. They weren't "clicking" this morning. Maybe it was only fantasy that had brought about the "click" last night. Disappointment cramped her heart.

She couldn't stay in his bed if he didn't respect the person she was.

"I can dress myself, Peter. I was just checking with you what would be suitable for the occasion."

He grimaced, annoyed at not having read the stand she was making. The laser blue eyes softened with apologetic appeal. "I only meant to smooth the way, not offend you, Erin. I didn't want you to feel out of place with the people who'll be there."

Protecting her?

The knots in her stomach loosened. That wasn't so bad. But the means of doing it was unacceptable. And there could be another motive behind his intention to put her in designer clothes. "You think I might shame you in front of them?" she challenged, watching his eyes to see if she'd hit a chord of pride.

Cinderella was fine for the bedroom but not to be paraded out in public?

His chin lifted in dismissive scorn. "I wouldn't care if you wear jeans." A cynical mockery glittered in his eyes. "It's the women who enjoy pecking other women apart. It didn't seem like a good idea to subject you to that, but if you can let it float over your head…"

"Fine!" A joyous relief poured into a smile so wide Peter looked as though he was completely thrown by it. "What time is it?" she asked.

"Almost nine," he answered somewhat absently.

"And what time do we have to be at the races?"

"About noon."

"I can do it." She hurled off the bedclothes, leapt out of bed and headed for a door, which stood ajar and obviously led to an ensuite bathroom. "Would you call me a taxi, Peter?" she tossed over her shoulder. "I'll be showered and dressed, ready to go in fifteen minutes."

"Go where?" He was on his feet, ready to take preventative action if he didn't like her reply.

Definitely a warrior, Erin thought, happily revelling in the secure knowledge that Peter Ramsey was not about to accept an ending to their relationship at this point and didn't care what anyone else thought of it.

"To David Jones in Elizabeth Street," she instructed. It was the classiest department store in Sydney. A couple of hours' shopping would see her dressed to the nines, nobody's fool at Randwick Racecourse. "You can pick me up at the taxi rank outside the store at eleven-thirty."

Peter's whole body clenched with frustration as she walked towards the bathroom, her black silky bed-mussed hair tumbling over her shoulders, the sexy curve of her spine drawing his gaze down to the even sexier derriere, its voluptuous sway reminding him of how provocatively exciting it had been last night. And the supple strength in those long legs…

winding around him, inviting, inciting a possession which she now denied.

You don't own me.

He'd meant to have her again this morning. The sight of her stretching so sensuously had paused him short of the bed, desire for her kicking in so strongly he was amazed by how deeply she stirred him. Then seeing her initial shock at the recollection of where she was, he'd thought a quick assurance that what they'd shared was not a one-night aberration on his part would please her. The hell of it was, he still wasn't sure he'd recovered the ground he'd lost with the clothes issue.

You don't own me.

The urge to stride into the bathroom and *make* her his again was burning through him— kiss her until passion exploded between them and she was happy for them to spend the whole day in bed together. Forget the damned horse and its maiden race! He didn't want anything getting in the way of what he'd found with Erin Lavelle.

But his rational mind warned that sex might not hold her. His wealth wouldn't hold her, either. There'd been no lure whatsoever in having designer gear freely showered on her. Quite the contrary. She hadn't liked that idea one bit. Hadn't even flirted with it for a moment. Erin Lavelle was up and running her way and that proud streak of independence in her was not about to bend.

Okay, so roll with her plan.

But no taxi.

He'd drive her to David Jones himself, talk with her on the way, make sure she wasn't running out on him. Peter frowned over that thought as he strode into his dressing room to throw on some clothes. Women invariably hung onto him as long as they could. Why was he feeling a lack of confidence in Erin's interest in him?

Because she was different.

Everything about her was different.

Which made it new to him.

And undoubtedly he was new to her, too.

Preschool teachers did not normally social-ise with billionaires. If she had reservations about that this morning—seeing no real future for this relationship—he had to allay them, because one thing was certain in his mind. He didn't want her walking out of his life. Not at this point.

Erin was surprised and pleased that Peter had decided to drive her into the city centre himself—an unnecessary double journey since he'd be picking her up later. She happily thought he wanted to spend the time with her, though once they were on their way, she noticed he wasn't particularly relaxed. In fact, his hands had a knuckle tight grip on the steering wheel.

Had he changed his mind about taking her to the races, introducing her to his social circle? Was he about to excuse himself— impulse shouldn't be carried too far? Maybe he felt guilty about her spending money on dressing up for him and was about to stop it before she was out of pocket. It was okay for him to be needlessly extravagant on a whim but letting her invest in a relationship that was going nowhere…

His silence fed the churning in her mind. When he finally spoke, Erin was gearing herself up to accept *the end* with as much grace as she could muster.

"About last night…" He darted a sharp look of concern at her. "I don't usually forget about protection…"

Protection!

Not rejection.

Relief billowed over her inner turmoil. She didn't want it to end here. She really didn't.

"It's okay," she swiftly assured him. "You won't get trapped into unplanned fatherhood with me, Peter. I'm on the pill."

Had been since she was sixteen. Her early teens had been plagued by irregular and very severe periods and she had no wish to suffer them again. The pill provided a regular monthly cycle, giving her peace of mind from being caught out in a desperately embarrassing flooding situation, not to mention the onset of almost intolerable pain.

A horrid thought occurred to her. "That's not to say I'm madly promiscuous. In case you're wondering, you don't have to worry about health issues, either." She took a deep breath and darted a sharp look of concern at him. "I hope *you're* not going to confess…"

"No." He flashed a reassuring smile. "I promise you I'm clean."

"Good!"

It certainly *was* good to have that settled.

She frowned over her reckless behaviour. "I should have thought of it last night."

"No harm done," he tossed at her, the smile still lingering even after he'd returned his attention to the traffic ahead.

Erin sighed away the load of tension he'd just lightened. Of course, he'd want such a serious issue raised and disposed of. They'd played a dangerous game last night. Luckily they hadn't been punished for it.

"Do you want to be a mother sometime in the future?" he asked in a tone of casual interest.

Erin took heart from the question. It didn't sound as though he was working up to bidding her goodbye just yet. "I would love to have children but I don't really see it happening," she said wryly.

"Why not?"

"Well, as I said last night, I think a solid marriage is the best environment for bringing up children and I'm not sure I'm cut out to be good wife material."

He shot her a quizzical look. "Define that for me."

"Oh, you know." She couldn't stop herself from mocking his need for an explanation. "Being subordinate to a husband. Having to give up part of me to get along with him. Seems to me it's never the other way around."

He frowned. "Sounds like you've had some disappointing personal experiences. How old are you, Erin?"

"I passed the big three zero almost a year ago," she answered flippantly, refusing to let that bother her. Life was to be lived, no matter what.

"So the biological clock is ticking," he muttered.

"Can't stop that," she agreed. No one had control over time. "How old are you, Peter?"

"Thirty-five."

"Then you must have had quite a few disappointing personal experiences, too."

"Click!" he said, throwing a wide dazzling grin at her.

Erin's heartbeat did its own clickety-click. Peter Ramsey was an absolutely gorgeous man. She was loving this experience with him. No doubt disappointment would come sooner or later, but until it did…

"To me the ideal marriage is a true partnership," he said. "Two people complementing each other, not competing for top billing."

"Ever seen that ideal in practice?" she challenged.

He nodded. "My parents. My sister and her husband. Though there are different aspects to their marriages. My mother might appear subordinate to my father, but she is very serious, very caring about her charity work and Dad respects and supports her desire to help, to make a difference. He doesn't demand that she always be at his side, looking after his needs. On the other hand, Charlotte and Damien are two like minds, sharing everything. Both have very solid marriages."

He spoke with such warmth about his family, Erin couldn't help feeling a stab of envy. "That's nice. You're very lucky, Peter."

"No." He shook his head. "*They* are. They found the right partners."

She looked at him curiously. "So which kind of marriage would you envisage for yourself, the first or the second?"

It could be possible for her to fit into the first mould, she was thinking. No way the second.

"I think if you find the person you want to spend your life with, you work it out from there."

"Hmm…that's an interesting theory, Peter." She smiled at him. "Meanwhile you're hanging loose."

He laughed and a hot blast of sexy blue twinkles zipped from his eyes and tingled all over her. "Not so loose at the moment," he drawled, leaving Erin in a ridiculously blissful state of exhilaration.

The parting of the ways was not going to happen today.

Peter Ramsey still wanted her.

Her prince...

She didn't care how different their worlds were. In fact, it would be fascinating to have a little taste of his today, so it was worth making the effort to fit in as well as she could, not create any awkward waves. Just being with him was making her feel anything was possible between them.

He drove around the northern end of Hyde Park and pulled up behind the taxi rank in Elizabeth Street. Illegal to park, so with engine idling, he reached across to squeeze one of her hands, his bright blue gaze seriously commanding. "Don't blow your budget on this, Erin. It really doesn't matter. Okay?"

"Okay." She smiled at his caring. "I'll just satisfy my female pride."

He smiled at her levity, pleased that she wasn't too concerned about the people she'd meet with him at Randwick. "Go to it. I'll be back here at eleven-thirty."

"I won't keep you waiting," she promised, and quickly alighted from the car.

Having waved him off, Erin hurried down to the pedestrian crossing which would take her directly to David Jones. Her dress from last night drew a few looks. It wasn't exactly morning wear. It could be put in a bag once she changed into whatever she bought. The great thing about David Jones was it could provide the lot; classy clothes and accessories, beautician, hair-stylist, manicurist. By eleven-thirty, she was going to look like a million dollars for Peter Ramsey and she didn't care about the cost.

Why should she?

The royalties on her books had made her one

of the wealthiest authors in the world. One of the reasons, she suspected, her editor wanted a more personal as well as a professional connection with her. Money did make people more attractive to the opposite sex. Though her success had drawn quite a lot of nasty envy, as well.

She didn't have to wear that with Peter.

Different worlds.

Maybe that wasn't bad.

Maybe…

Erin quelled the heart-fluttering hope before it took really wild wings. Today she was going to Randwick to watch horse-races with Peter Ramsey and that was adventure enough. Plus right now she had the fun of shopping to knock his socks off.

A happy day.

Silly to start wanting too much.

CHAPTER SEVEN

PETER had to stop the BMW at the pedestrian crossing from Hyde Park to St Mary's Cathedral, just short of where he had dropped Erin this morning. The dashboard clock read eleven thirty-one. He'd timed his arrival almost perfectly. Was she waiting for him?

He checked the sidewalk that curved down to Elizabeth Street. His quickly scanning gaze caught sight of a woman standing in the shade of an overhanging tree, just past the end of the taxi rank—a stunningly attired woman who looked as if she'd stepped out of the fashion pages of *Vogue* magazine.

Was it Erin?

A very stylish black hat dipped over her face, making her identity uncertain for a moment, though the hair was right, the body shape was right. Her head turned towards him and his heart thumped with a great leap of excitement. It *was* her. She saw the blue BMW, smiled, waved, moved out from the shade towards the edge of the sidewalk, ready to join him.

The dress she wore was a sleeveless, silky wraparound, a deep jade-green with big black polka dots. A wide black leather belt held it in place and accentuated the smallness of her waist and the curve of her hips. The crossover bodice gave a teasing hint of cleavage, and as she walked, the skirt flapped open enough to give a provocative glimpse of thigh. Black high-heels with thin straps around her ankles completed an outfit that was all sexy woman.

A hot rush of blood to his groin warned him he'd be in serious discomfort if he didn't lift his mind off the desire she aroused. The car behind him honked impatience. The traffic lights had turned green. He quickly accelerated, signalling his intention to pull over to the sidewalk, and doing so right beside Erin.

She held up a large black and white signature David Jones carry-bag. "Can I put this in the boot of the car?"

"Sure can." He pressed the central unlocking button, then leaned over to open the passenger door for her.

Having stowed the bag in the boot compartment, she slid into the seat beside him, another flash of legs raising his body temperature again. She quickly closed the door, grabbed the seat-belt and the lush fullness of her breasts was temptingly emphasised as the belt was whipped between them and fastened.

"We're off!" she declared, lifting a face that glowed with happy anticipation.

No. We're on, Peter thought, a fierce wave of feeling driving a determination to make

Erin Lavelle realise she was *his* woman. That didn't mean owning her. It meant he was the man in her life.

"Do I pass muster?" she asked as he put the car into gear, ready to ease into the traffic.

The note of vulnerability in her voice reminded him of what it must have cost her to look the part of his companion at Randwick. He didn't want her feeling nervous about appearing at his side in public and she certainly had no reason to be.

"You look fabulous, Erin," he quickly assured her, smiling his appreciation of how incredibly striking she was. "Every guy at the race-course will be jealous of me."

She laughed her pleasure in the compliment. "Thank you." Her gorgeous green eyes skated over him, taking in the mid-grey suit with its darker grey pinstripe, the white shirt and gold silk tie. "You look fabulous, too."

The husky words ended in a sharp intake of breath and a long sigh as though she needed to relieve a tightness in her chest. Peter was suffering a fair amount of physical tightness himself. He concentrated on driving because there was no other optional action at the moment, but he was acutely aware of the woman beside him, wanting her more than he could remember wanting any other woman.

"Are you the jealous type, Peter?" she asked in a wary tone.

"No." He threw her a teasing look. "You can strike jealousy off the list."

She looked startled. "What list?"

He grinned. "The bad husband material list you were citing this morning."

"Oh! I was not…I mean…" She floundered, embarrassed by having her general observations applied so personally to him.

She definitely wasn't measuring him up as a possible husband.

Was a marriage to him too pie-in-the-sky to her mind?

He didn't feel she was anti-marriage, just distrustful of how the commitment was worked.

No problem with sharing his bed, so sharing his life had to be the stumbling block. From what she'd said, the idea of sharing any man's life was not an attractive proposition, and his certainly carried the penalty of public scrutiny. Though she hadn't backed off from that aspect, probably spending far more than she could really afford on clothes to be with him at Randwick today.

Peter wondered how far he could push the relationship, how far Erin Lavelle would let it be pushed before her strong sense of independence kicked in and cut him out. He didn't think his wealth counted for anything with her. In fact, far from being a gold-star attraction, that might well be a stumbling block, too.

"It was you who brought up the subject of marriage, Peter," she said, still discomfited by his husband-list comment.

"Marriage and motherhood," he readily conceded, intent on stirring some more telling reactions.

"Right! So we've covered that ground."

She was drawing a line of finality under it.

"I've never been to the races," she quickly stated. "Tell me what to expect. Tell me about your horse."

She made it easy to oblige her, flooding him with eager questions, listening to his answers so she could hit off them, broadening her inquiry into the whole business of horse-racing. In fact, her concentrated interest made it a pleasure to give her the knowledge she sought, and by the time they reached Randwick Race-course, Peter was thinking he'd never been interviewed so intelligently on a subject.

Her lively curiosity continued over lunch in the directors' dining room and in the champagne bar afterwards. The people they met—

friends, acquaintances and associates of his—all responded very positively to the happy energy she emitted. It was impossible not to like her.

Her smile, the gorgeous green eyes sparkling with fascinated interest, the way she listened, focussing so directly on the person who was speaking to her and soaking in every word that was said…the men were all charmed by her, the women intrigued, surreptitiously eyeing her over, half of them probably wanting to find fault and frustrated at not finding anything to criticise.

He knew what they were thinking—*Who is this Erin Lavelle?*

The wife of one of the race-course directors actually mulled over the name out loud. "Erin Lavelle… I'm sure I've read about you somewhere. I just can't think of the connection. Such a pretty name. Are you an actress or something?"

Erin laughed at the idea, shaking her head.

"I'm simply lucky enough to be Peter's companion today." She hugged his arm, her eyes flirtatiously engaging his, deflecting any further pursuit of her personal identity.

Peter got the message that she didn't want him to give out information on her background so he deftly turned the conversation away from what might be a sensitive issue to her in this company.

Was it another fantasy, he wondered, being his mystery companion for the day?

As they moved away, heading for the members' terrace to watch the races, he aimed a quizzical smile at her. "Are you worried that I might be uncomfortable about having it known that you're a preschool teacher I met in a public park?"

He wouldn't be, Erin thought. He'd probably be amused by the reactions such a statement would arouse. But would he be as amused to find himself with a woman who was not a nobody? If she'd told that director's wife why the name of Erin Lavelle was familiar to her, revealed the fame she had in her own field, this easy comfort zone she and Peter currently occupied could have been blown sky-high.

She hadn't wanted to risk that—people gushing over her in public, ignoring the man who was giving her this special day, making him feel stupid for not knowing the truth about her. The truth would have to be told soon enough. But not yet. She didn't want him to look at her differently. She liked what they were sharing right now, didn't want anything to spoil it.

"I have the right to keep my private life private, Peter," she said quietly. It was best that way. She hated all the fuss that came with being *the author.* And the men she'd been with hadn't liked it, either, being put in the shade of her success.

"The longer you're with me, the less chance you have of that, Erin," Peter warned seriously.

She heaved a rueful sigh, realising that his high profile would inevitably stir interest in any woman at his side. Her eyes appealed for his forebearance. "It's no one else's business how we met or what we're doing together. Let's just take one day at a time, Peter."

Peter's protective instincts rose instantly to the fore as he read the vulnerability in her eyes. No way would he let anyone badger Erin about her background, making her feel not up to his status. Though her obvious insecurity about how long they'd be together stirred an even stronger determination that this connection with Erin Lavelle was not going to be a one-day wonder.

"Well, today is race day," he said lightly, "so let's go and watch the races."

They found good seats on the members' terrace and Erin relaxed, eager to soak up more new knowledge. He explained the coloured silks of the jockeys as the horses were paraded out to the starting gates. She seemed totally entranced by the scene, sitting with her hands in her lap, her body leaning forward, her gaze trained on the horses as they raced around the course.

She didn't leap up in excitement as they turned for the gallop to the winning post. The crowd on the terrace was in its usual uproar but she simply sat quietly, and Peter had the uneasy feeling her mind had slipped to another place and she was there by herself, not with him or anyone else. The race finished and she didn't even seem aware of the bustling aftermath—people going off to get drinks, celebrating their winnings or commiserating over their losses.

"Erin…"

No response.

He reached over and touched her hands. Her head jerked towards him, eyes wide and startled.

"Where were you?" he asked.

"Oh!" Hot colour whooshed into her cheeks. Embarrassed confusion in her eyes. "I'm sorry. I didn't mean to drift off. I just do sometimes," she rattled out apologetically.

Did she have some mental problem?

"It's nothing to do with you, Peter," she swiftly assured him. "You've been marvellous company. It was watching the horses. They're so beautiful and it started me thinking…"

She hesitated, frowning, and he sensed a deep reluctance to reveal the inner workings of her mind. Instinctively recognising a barrier that had to faced, crossed if possible, Peter pushed for an understanding of what it entailed.

"Erin, I don't have to be the centre of your attention. I'm just curious about what did captivate it so exclusively."

She heaved a sigh, following it up with a wry grimace. "I have a vivid imagination, Peter. Sometimes it just takes off. I know it's a bit disconcerting for the people I'm with. I don't mean to block them out. Please just excuse it. Okay?" She gave him a blindingly brilliant smile. "I'm right back in your world now."

As opposed to *her* world? Which she thought he couldn't, wouldn't share?

"What was going on in your imagination?" he pressed.

Her eyes instantly took on a guarded look. It told him she was mentally backing off even before she voiced the dismissal in her mind. "I was just playing with an idea. Let's leave it at that." Then she was on her feet, emitting a sense of urgency. "I really need to go to the ladies' room. Will you excuse me?"

"Of course."

He stood to accompany her part of the way but she was already rushing off, leaving Peter feeling that he'd somehow lost that round with Erin Lavelle. Though she had given him a valuable insight into how she viewed this encounter with him. They came from separate worlds and to her mind, it wasn't feasible that the two would mix, so any long-term relation-ship with him was not on the cards.

She might be right.

But Peter was not about to give up on what he felt with this woman. The sense that he'd be *missing out* was stronger than ever.

Wonderful winged horses were flying through Erin's mind as she quickly negotiated her way to the ladies' room—five of them: white, grey, chestnut, dark brown and black, with beauti-fully coloured wings, like butterflies. The Mythical horses of...of...Mirrima. That sounded right. They were going to make a marvellous, magical story.

She'd been constructing the opening verse for it when Peter had called her out of her creative reverie. This wasn't the time or place for her to go on with it but she wanted to get these first thoughts into her notebook for later.

Luckily she had transferred everything from last night's handbag to the new black one she'd bought this morning. It was automatic—never going anywhere without a notebook and pen.

As soon as she reached the ladies' room, she had them out, writing down the ideas that had come to her. They were exciting and she had to quell the urge to keep playing with them. Peter Ramsey was her top priority today and she didn't want to put him off her. If she hadn't already by tripping somewhere else in her mind.

Not good, Erin chided herself. She'd had the amazing luck to meet an amazing man and what he'd given her so far was much better than any imaginary world. Stupid to put it at risk by acting oddly. Their differences would no doubt end it soon enough, but she'd much prefer it to be later than sooner.

"Giving Peter Ramsey a rating in your little black book?"

The mocking drawl snapped Erin's head

around. A beautiful blonde, spectacularly dressed in a Colette Dinnigan creation with a gorgeous fascinator pinned to her hair, was eyeing her with such malicious spite, Erin was momentarily speechless with shock.

"So where did he find you?" the blonde bored in.

Erin swiftly found wits enough to say. "I beg your pardon. Have we met?"

"Since you don't run with the usual crowd and Peter has been steering you clear of me today, no, we haven't. I'm Alicia Hemmings, Peter's very recent ex."

And obviously smarting from rejection or she wouldn't have sought this confrontation. Erin couldn't help wondering what had caused Peter to end the relationship. Had the designer clothes come from him? Had Alicia Hemmings got too greedy, wanting more and more?

"I'm sorry," she said. "I know nothing about this."

"You're obviously very new on the scene," Alicia jeered.

"Yes," Erin agreed. "I haven't been in Australia for quite a while." That left everything nicely vague, nothing for this woman to seize on and tear apart.

"Brought you back from London with him, did he?"

She wasn't going to stop, though whatever satisfaction she was looking for, Erin wasn't about to give it. "This really is none of your business, Alicia," she said bluntly. "If you'll excuse me…"

"No doubt he swept you off your feet, being a billionaire and all that goes with it," Alicia mocked as Erin hastily stowed the notebook and pen in her bag. "But let me tell you he's a strait-laced bastard who wants his pound of flesh unblemished, so better give up any dirty little habits you have if you want to hang onto him."

Curiosity got the better of Erin's sense of

discretion. "I don't know what you mean," tripped off her tongue.

"Oh, come on. The London party scene is rife with ecstasy and cocaine. I've been there, done that."

"And Peter doesn't do drugs?"

"Squeaky clean, darling. A total control freak. And no patience with anyone who isn't." A nasty smile curled her mouth. "Just thought I'd warn you what you're in for."

"Thank you," Erin said, curiosity completely satisfied.

Apparently Alicia was satisfied enough with having delivered her piece of poison to let Erin make her exit from the ladies' room without throwing any more nasty darts. No doubt she had been all sweetness and light with Peter, doing her utmost to hang onto him, and was bitter about having been caught out indulging herself with designer chemicals. He was well rid of her, Erin thought. And she didn't mind one bit about Peter being a control freak—being inclined that way herself—as long as he didn't try to control her.

It was one thing to choose, quite another to be pressured into complying with someone else's will.

Peter had been completely fair in his dealings with her so far. Even last night on the balcony of his Bondi Beach penthouse…she paused for a moment, her thighs squeezing together at the exciting memory of being touched so erotically, touching him, her stomach contracting as her mind relived being totally out of control with the wild, hungry passion he'd evoked in her.

Her heart actually quivered as she caught sight of him breaking from a group of people, his vivid blue eyes trained purposefully on her as he made his way to where she stood. Her entire body seemed to hum with pleasure at just this minor connection with him. He was such a magnificent man, and as fabulous as he looked in his superb suit, Erin couldn't help mentally stripping him of it, revelling again in his splendid physique. She wanted him. Again and again and again.

Her consciousness was so swamped by the desire he stirred, she didn't pick up his tension until he was right in front of her, his eyes searching hers with sharp intensity. "Are you okay, Erin?"

"Yes, I'm fine," she quickly assured him, belatedly recalling her distraction with the horses and hoping he would let it slide.

"You weren't subjected to an unpleasant scene in the ladies' room?" The hard, ruthless edge to his voice woke her up to the fact he was bristling from his failure to protect her from his ex.

"Oh, that!" She smiled, relieved at hearing the different concern, and loving his caring for her. "No problem, Peter. Though I'd have to say your ex is not a very nice person."

His grimace was both rueful and apologetic. "I saw Alicia hot-footing it to the ladies' room but was too far away to run interference."

"Don't worry about it." She stepped forward, hooking her arm around his. "Let's go back to the terrace. It must be time for the next race."

"You're not bothered by anything she said?" he asked, falling in with the suggestion and hugging her arm tightly to his side as they moved on together.

She slanted him a teasing look. "Should I be?"

He frowned. "I like to get things sorted, Erin. Clear the air."

His tension hadn't eased. Erin realised a blithe dismissal of her encounter with Alice Hemmings was not relieving it. Peter didn't want to be left wondering about what had transpired between them. Which was fair enough, given that the idea of being bad-mouthed behind one's back wasn't exactly palatable.

"As far as I'm concerned, it was all good,"

she assured him, rolling her eyes in amusement as she elaborated. "Alicia called you a squeaky-clean control freak who doesn't tolerate dirty little habits like recreational drug-taking."

His mouth took on an ironic quirk. "You thought that was good?"

"Well, since squeaky-clean certainly appeals, and I have no inclination to tamper with how my brain works with mind-altering drugs, the only question mark hovers over the control bit, but I haven't found you freaky yet, so I'm willing to ride with my own judgement until it's proved wrong," she flipped at him.

"Thank you," he said mock seriously, then laughed as though delighted with how her brain worked, his blue eyes sparkling so brightly, so appreciatively, Erin felt his pleasure in her filling her heart with happiness, making it swell with happiness.

And the realisation hit her...she was falling

in love with Peter Ramsey. It was more than a strong physical attraction. She wasn't going to be able to write off this connection with him as *an experience* and just move on with her own life. She wanted him with an intensity that was suddenly frightening.

Panic swirled through her mind.

She wouldn't fit into his life.

He wouldn't fit into hers.

Then overriding the panic came a fierce resolution.

Take now, and spin now out for as long as it feels right.

CHAPTER EIGHT

THE irritating buzz of the bedside telephone woke him. Peter quickly reached out and snatched up the receiver, not wanting Erin to be disturbed from her sleep. It had been a long night of the most sensual sex he'd ever experienced. The desire they stirred in each other was incredibly mutual and he wanted her to stay in his bed as long as he could keep her there.

The clock-radio read one minute past eight. His mother was nattering away on the telephone line. He muffled the voice noise with his hand as he slid swiftly from Erin's side and strode out of the bedroom, quietly closing the door behind him. He took a deep breath to quell his sharp annoyance at being called this early on a Sunday morning. If it wasn't his mother...

He lifted the receiver to his ear and couldn't quite keep an impatient terseness out of his voice as he demanded, "What's up, Mum? Some emergency?"

A blank silence, then, "Haven't you been listening, Peter?"

"I'm barely awake," he said on an exasperated sigh.

"Then you don't know that you and Erin Lavelle are front page news? They've even used a full colour photograph!"

"Oh, for pity's sake! Haven't they got better things to report than spotting me with a new woman." He remembered photographers clicking away when his horse had won its maiden race and in the excitement of the win, he hadn't thought to shield Erin from them.

"But she isn't just any new woman, is she, dear?" his mother drawled pointedly.

"What do you mean by that?" he growled. Had the gossip merchants spun some stupid story about her? Something that would embarrass her at the preschool?

"I'd love to meet her, Peter. Do bring her out to lunch with us today."

His mother's enthusiasm struck an extremely false note. She didn't hand out invitations at the drop of a hat. "Why do you want to meet her, Mum?" he asked warily. "We've only known each other a couple of days." Usually he had to be attached to a woman for months before his mother began taking an interest in her.

"Darling, you go to any children's wards in any hospital and Erin Lavelle's books are there by the dozen. Her stories whisk even the sickest children off to a better place. They love them. Why wouldn't I want to meet the author who can make them forget their misery?"

The author…

It took Peter's mind several dazed moments

to connect with this stunning information. Erin was not a preschool teacher. Her aunt ran the school and Erin had been with her in the park, but she'd been there to tell the children a story—a story they loved—a story she had written herself!

She knew he had assumed she worked at the school. Why not set him straight? He'd brought up the Princess of Evermore at the Thai restaurant—*one of her favourite stories,* she'd said—the perfect opening to tell him the truth. And yesterday at Randwick, when the director's wife had queried her on her name, she could have explained to him afterwards that Erin Lavelle meant more than just a name to a hell of a lot of other people. Or when the horses had set her imagination running…she could have laid it out then. He'd *asked* her to.

He hated deception. What point was there in Erin hiding what she did? He wouldn't have thought less of her. Yet she had deliberately held back on revealing her full identity. Over and over again!

"Peter?" his mother pushed, impatient with his silence.

He dragged his mind back to the lunch invitation. "I'll have to discuss it with Erin, Mum."

"Of course. Get back to me as soon as you can, dear."

He re-entered his bedroom, checked that Erin was still fast asleep, grabbed a pair of shorts from his dressing room, pulled them on, then moved out again to ride the elevator down to the lobby of the apartment complex where he could pick up the Sunday newspaper that had uncovered Erin's literary career.

No mistaking it.

The front page carried a full colour photograph of Erin stroking the horse that had won its maiden race—his horse—with himself standing by, smiling at her. The dip of her hat partially hid her face. Had she been aware of cameras clicking and turned aside to maintain privacy? Though apparently her name had been enough to set bells ringing in some reporter's head.

The headline read—*Famous Reclusive Author, Erin Lavelle, Outed By Peter Ramsey.*

Famous...not to him because he'd taken no interest in children's books since he was a child himself.

Reclusive...that could explain her reluctance to open up about herself, but why was she reclusive? Most authors surely courted publicity to promote their books.

Once back in his penthouse, Peter took the newspaper into his study and flipped over the pages to the cover story. Erin Lavelle's first book had been phenomenally successful world-wide, spawning a huge market for character toys and games from the story she had created. Subsequent books had enormous print-runs, selling out almost as soon as they hit the shelves. But she had not granted any interviews since the flurry of publicity over the first book, preferring to keep her life absolutely private. Her agent had quoted her as saying, "My stories speak for themselves."

There was the usual garbage about him—women he'd been involved with. According to the reporter, only his billionaire status could have drawn Erin Lavelle out in public with him. Which was ridiculous. She had to be very wealthy in her own right. More likely she hadn't realised that being at Randwick with him would put her privacy at risk.

Different worlds…

Needing to know more about hers, he switched on his computer and did an Internet search on her name. She did not have a personal Web site but he got hits on her publisher's site, her agent's site and the marketing company, which had profitably exploited the popularity of her stories. Erin Lavelle was big business for a lot of people. Yet rather than bask in the spotlight of fame she had retreated to live in the shadows.

She wasn't going to like being front page news. *I have the right to keep my private life private.* Fair enough, he reluctantly conceded, but the fact that she had kept her fame hidden from him—repeatedly—despite the intimacy they had shared—could mean only one thing. She viewed him—had from the start—as a very temporary item in her life, a brief side play that was never going to move to centre stage.

Frustration welled up in him. He wanted answers and he wanted them right now. Tense, angry, determined on confrontation, he grabbed the newspaper and charged upstairs with it, flinging the bedroom door open, only to be frustrated further by finding his bed empty of the woman he wanted to pin down.

Had she done a flit while he was in the study?

No, her clothes were still strewn around the

floor. They'd been so hot for each other after the races, the only thought they'd had about clothes was to get them off. Did she only want him for the sex?

"Erin!"

He heard the harsh demand in his voice and told himself to calm down. Nothing was ever gained with an intemperate manner. She had to be in the bathroom. Any moment now she would come out…

The ensuite door opened.

She stepped into the bedroom, a towel draped around her body, droplets of water still clinging to her bare arms and legs, and her rainbow smile beaming at him, churning him up even further.

"Hi! I was just drying off. Woke up, found you gone, thought I'd have a shower." Her gaze dropped to his hand. "Been out buying a newspaper?"

Everything about her seemed so natural. The urge to just shunt aside this whole identity issue and sweep her back into bed with him pumped through his body. But his mind insisted she had lied to him—lied by omission. How far would she have taken the deception?

"My mother called. Asked me to bring you to lunch with her," he said, wanting to see Erin's reaction to the invitation.

"Your mother?" It was a shock. Then came a puzzled frown. "When did you speak to her about me?"

It was impossible to tell if she was pleased or not at the prospect of meeting his family. Peter gave up trying to read her mind and tossed the newspaper on the bed, the front page carrying its own glaring message.

"She saw this!"

This...

Erin felt his anger. It was like an iron hand squeezing her heart. She knew something was terribly wrong even before her gaze fastened on the full page photograph and its telling caption. Then the realisation hit her with sickening certainty that the wonderful idyll with Peter Ramsey was over.

He didn't like her being a famous author.

He didn't like her being made the focal point of whatever story had been concocted in this newspaper, taking the limelight he was undoubtedly used to.

It always got to men.

They pretended it didn't for a while but it always did.

A savagely mocking voice told her Peter Ramsey was no different, despite the ego-bulwark of his billions. He wasn't big enough to accept everything about her, after all.

She flicked him a wry look. "I guess you liked the idea of Cinderella better."

"Not particularly," he shot back at her, his face hardening at her comment on him. "I prefer honesty to role-playing."

"You started the role-playing, Peter," she reminded him. "Offering to be my prince. And I let myself be sucked into it because I really did think you might be."

A muscle in his cheek contracted. His eyes blazed with fierce resentment. "You knew what you were getting, Erin. I didn't bypass any important facts about me."

"Who really knows anybody?" she muttered derisively.

There were always—*always*—things hidden— things that came out to bite you when some emotional trigger was hit. She'd been subjected to this kind of angry man pride before and knew there was no fixing it, short of giving up writing and becoming a satellite to *his* interests. Erin gritted her teeth. Not even for this man would she give up her essential self.

She turned aside to gather up her clothes, and the David Jones bag that held what she'd worn on Friday night. Better to make her exit in the latter outfit, since yesterday's made her too recognisable to anyone who'd seen the newspaper photograph. Which reminded her of the invitation it had instantly brought.

"I bet your mother wouldn't have wanted to meet me if I wasn't *the author*," she slung at Peter who was watching her, his hands clenched at his sides, wanting to fight, but thwarted by a truth he couldn't deny.

Having picked up everything she needed Erin headed back towards the ensuite bathroom. Her legs were like jelly but she forced them to take the necessary steps away from the tension-laden atmosphere of the bedroom—a bedroom that had been full of glorious pleasure last night, but which promised only pain this morning.

"Damn it, Erin! You could have told me!" he hurled after her.

She glanced back over her shoulder, her chin lifting defiantly at his angry challenge.

"That would have changed your view of me. As it just has."

"Blocking out a big part of you creates a false view," he argued vehemently. "Why not give me the full picture?"

"Because one way or another it has tainted every relationship I've had since the roller-coaster success of my first book." Her eyes mocked his lack of understanding. "I avoid the zoo, Peter, because I don't like being the performing monkey, and that's all people like your mother want of me."

"That's not true! My mother would have respected any line you drew."

"Then I hope you'll do the same, because I'm drawing the line on us right now."

She stepped into the bathroom and quickly closed the door, leaning her head against it as a wave of nausea rolled through her. She hated being *the author.* Hated it, hated it, hated it. Yet there was no turning back the clock and she couldn't deny that she loved writing the stories—the excitement of coming up with a new idea, the joy she had in putting the right words together, creating the rhythm that made the story flow so captivatingly.

It was a big part of her.

But there was the other part—the lonely child who'd wanted someone to love and cherish her. *The author* had grown out of that child, spinning dreams where whatever she wanted did happen. But it had never happened in real life. And wasn't going to happen with Peter Ramsey.

Miserably accepting the inevitable, Erin pulled herself together enough to get dressed and stow the Randwick clothes in the carry bag. As she transferred the contents of the new black handbag to the tan one, her notebook reminded her that at least she had something to move onto. The Mythical Horses of Mirrima should consume her attention for months, giving her a fairly effective escape from brooding over broken dreams.

She took a deep breath, bracing herself to face Peter one last time. *Make it quick,* her mind dictated. *Be dignified, don't cry, and don't get into any further argument. It's over.*

He wasn't in the bedroom.

Having expected to run straight into another nerve-tearing confrontation, Erin paused to take stock of this different situation. Was he waiting for her in the living room downstairs? Had he decided there was nothing to be gained from fighting over something that couldn't be changed anyhow?

A heaviness settled on her heart as her gaze drifted out to the balcony where…

He was there!

Her stomach instantly contracted.

Was he remembering what they'd done on Friday night, how they'd felt?

He was still wearing only a pair of shorts, his

back turned to her, looking out to sea, hands gripping the railing. Every muscle of his powerful physique looked taut. So much strength—strength she had revelled in—yet he knew how to be gentle as well, and endearingly tender. The perfect lover for her.

Erin closed her eyes as beautiful memories clutched her own body, sending quivers down her thighs, stiffening her nipples, bringing a moist heat to her sex. She would never forget this man. What they'd shared had been very special. It didn't matter that it had been driven by fantasy. The physical intimacy had been intensely real.

If she walked out there and touched him as she had on their first night…could he—would he—put the author thing aside?

Another fantasy, Erin, her mind savagely chided. It lay between them now. Nothing would be the same as before.

Heaving a desolate sigh, she forced her eyes

open. Peter hadn't moved. Was his back a message in itself?—*I'm out of your way. Go!*

It was probably the best thing to do, but she couldn't bring herself to sneak out without at least saying goodbye. Peter had given her much of himself and that deserved some recognition and appreciation. He was a good man. He just wasn't accustomed to having his top gun status taken by a woman.

She walked over to the opened doorway to the balcony, close enough to speak, but leaving a fair distance between them. "Peter…" she called softly, hoping his anger had cooled a little.

He turned slowly, eyeing her up and down as he settled to leaning back against the railing, his arms folded forbiddingly across his magnificently sculptured chest. Her appearance in the green, lemon and lime dress did not ignite one spark of desire. It was patently clear that a wall of hard pride ensured she didn't reach him in any way whatsoever. Indeed, the blue eyes were so cold a little shiver ran down Erin's spine.

"Was going to a party on Friday night a lie, too?" he asked sardonically.

"Yes," she admitted. "I set out to make myself as attractive as I could, but you didn't seem to like what was probably too obvious an effort, so I made up an excuse for it."

He nodded, as though she was only confirming what he'd already worked out. "You wanted some playtime with me."

Erin frowned over his choice of words. "I wanted the man I'd met in the park to want me because I found him very attractive. I wasn't thinking in terms of *playtime*."

"You didn't give a real relationship between us a chance," he mocked accusingly. "You're drawing the line because it's not playtime anymore."

"I took the chance you gave me, Peter, because in my heart of hearts, I did want it to be real."

He shook his head. "You can't build anything real on deception. Every time I tried to make progress with you, you shut me out."

That was probably fair comment from his point of view, yet Erin knew only too well why she'd done what she'd done. "I was trying to hang onto what we had together. Just a man and a woman. Not the billionaire and the author."

Her sad irony was lost on him.

"But it always had an ending in your mind," he replied cuttingly. "You didn't trust me to take the author on board and deal with your world."

"I hoped you would," she said quietly, her whole body aching from the loss of that hope. He was attacking her on deception because he *didn't* want to deal with her world. It was easier to paint her black than to look into himself and acknowledge he wasn't big enough to take on all that she was.

He stared at her, the twin blue lasers of his eyes stabbing hard, transmitting his disbelief in the hope she had just expressed. Erin gave up, her hand lifting to communicate the futility of any further talk, gesturing her helplessness to save the situation.

"I'm sorry you imagined something different, Peter. I just wanted to thank you for all you did give me."

His mouth thinned into a grim line as though he was refusing to let what they'd shared be worth anything. Erin sensed he was too deeply into painting her black to even see there could be other colours.

"Goodbye," she said and turned away quickly, wanting to run, run so fast her heart would pump out the awful weight of misery it was carrying. Somehow she managed to hold her legs to a reasonably steady walk across the bedroom to the door, which would lead to her exit from his life.

She fiercely willed Peter to remain silent, to simply let her go.

He did.

It wasn't a good silence. It pulsed with violent feelings that were being forcibly repressed. Peter Ramsey felt ill-used by her and he hated it with a vengeance. Erin hated him feeling like that—she'd loved the man who had made love to her. But she couldn't change what was unchangeable and the fantasy was over.

There could be no transition to real life.

The billionaire and the author did not click.

CHAPTER NINE

H<small>ER</small> little fling…

Peter seethed over being cast for that role by Erin Lavelle. He couldn't see it any other way, given her readiness to leave him when the situation no longer suited her. Toy with *the prince* for a while, fulfil a few sexual fantasies, enjoy whatever entertainment he provides, but keep him in the box marked Playtime.

The infuriating part was all the signals had been there if he hadn't been so blindly arrogant about his own appeal to a Cinderella preschool teacher. Erin had dressed to bowl him over on Friday night and there'd not been the slightest hesitation over going to *his castle*.

Even her serene silence in the car on the drive out to Bondi Beach should have telegraphed he was doing precisely what she'd wanted of him. Why bother with conversation when the game was well and truly on?

Then the way she'd taken over out on the balcony…

All the pleasure she'd given him was soured by the knowledge that she had only been interested in having a physical relationship, and only on her own terms, as well.

Her proud refusal to be indebted to him over a set of clothes, the sharp warning, *You don't own me, Peter,* her evasion on the husband-list issue, the way she'd concentrated so much interest in horses and horse-racing, which could be of use to her as a writer—in fact, she'd obviously had some idea for a story yesterday afternoon—the whole encounter had been on her terms.

But the game was now up.

She'd closed the door on it and he wasn't about to contest her decision. In his whole life, no one had ever made him feel this small. Totally insignificant.

He waited until she had to be clear of the apartment complex, taking a taxi to wherever she lived—another fact withheld from him— then got himself ready to go to the gym, needing an outlet for the volcano of aggressive energy, which he'd somehow kept capped while Erin was calmly going about her departure.

Two hours later, after a punishing workout, Peter was leaving the gym when his cell phone rang. His mother's number on the screen reminded him of her luncheon invitation, which had completely slipped his mind. Cursing under his breath, he made the connection and offered his apology.

"Sorry, Mum. I should have got back to you before this. Can't do lunch today. Erin is not available."

"Oh!" A big sigh of disappointment. "I was so looking forward to meeting her. Can we arrange something else, Peter?"

He grimaced at the unwelcome suggestion though he probably should have anticipated it, given his mother's interest in *the author*. "I can't oblige on that, either. We had an argument this morning and it's all off between us," he said bluntly, not wanting to be pestered on the sore subject.

"Oh dear! Just when I thought you'd found someone really nice," his mother said wistfully. "There's so much heart in her stories…"

She hadn't shown much heart to him!

"…and the way they're told and illustrated," his mother babbled on. "She has to have a beautiful mind to think of such things. You must have felt attracted to her, Peter. She looks beautiful on the outside, too. Why on earth would you let her go?"

"Mum, it's a case of her letting me go. Okay?" he bit out, hating the necessity to spell that out.

"Why? What did you do to upset her?"

Like it was his fault!

Peter unclenched his teeth enough to say, "I really don't want to go into this."

"Was it the publicity? Didn't she realise that being with you would attract media attention?"

He reached his car which was parked handily at the street kerb outside the gym. "I said I don't want to go into this," he repeated emphatically. "Bye, Mum."

He broke the connection, tucked the small cell-phone in his shirt pocket, unlocked the BMW, sat himself in the driver's seat and decided he didn't want to go back to the apartment where memories of Erin were far too close. Yacht Club, he thought. Sailing might help get her out of his mind.

Over the next few weeks, Peter worked very hard at blocking Erin Lavelle out of his consciousness, pouring his energy into dealing with business during the day, carrying on with his usual social life at night, playing various sports at the weekend—squash, tennis, polo. He dismissed any questions about his relationship with her by saying Erin had wanted to know about horse-racing. End of story.

It was a lie—a self-protective lie.

And he felt uncomfortable with it.

Especially since he could not get her out of his mind.

He was blind to the attraction of any other woman. He didn't want anyone else in his bed. His mother's comment—beautiful inside and outside—began to haunt him, reminding him of all the things he'd liked about Erin. Maybe he'd made a mistake in reacting so negatively to what might have been a self-protective lie on her part. Hadn't there been a moment in the park when he'd felt a strong reluctance to reveal his own identity?

Just a man and a woman...

Erin sat in the chair behind her desk, staring at a blank monitor screen. There was no point in turning on the computer. No way could she get her head around work today. She didn't know why she was sitting here. Instinctive, probably, putting herself in the place where she was most comfortable, tapping out words on a keyboard. But there was only one mountainous word in her mind, blocking out the flow of any others.

Pregnant.

The shock of it drained her of any sense of purpose. She hadn't recognised the symptoms. How could she, knowing nothing about pregnancy, and not even suspecting such a cataclysmic cause to feeling *off?* She hadn't been sleeping well—too much churning over memories of Peter Ramsey. And eating too much comfort food, then feeling queasy in the morning.

It seemed reasonable to think her normal system was messed up when the contraceptive pill she'd been taking for years didn't produce the regular monthly period, but she'd decided to check it out with a doctor, uneasy with the idea of her body not responding as it should to what had always been reliable before.

Pregnant.

She was going to be a mother.

And Peter Ramsey was the father.

Never mind that the pill was ninety-nine percent safe from falling pregnant. Peter Ramsey had beaten that percentage in two nights of intense sexual action. Or her own body had treacherously welcomed him beyond the point of stopping anything, because what had been happening between them was so...so extraordinary.

But fantastic sex wasn't enough to make a relationship work. He didn't like *the author* taking over his spotlight. Not that she wanted it. She would have been perfectly happy standing in his shadow for the rest of her life. It was her evasion of publicity that had made her so newsworthy. But evasion would probably be impossible if she was appearing at his side, so the problem would never go away.

Neither would this one.

She was now faced with having his child.

And he would probably think she'd lied about being protected from pregnancy, too.

If she told him about it.

Could she keep this child a secret from him? They occupied such different worlds. In the normal course of events, they should never meet again. It was possible…or was it, given that someone somewhere would blab about Erin Lavelle having a child and it could end up being a news story that she had no control over.

Then if Peter put two and two together, the

warrior in him would fight her tooth and nail over custody, and everything could turn really, really nasty. He'd accuse her of more and more lies, hating her for shutting him out of where he had every right to be. That was definitely not a road to go down.

Besides, knowing how strongly Peter felt about fatherhood, hiding his child from him would never sit well on her conscience. It wasn't fair, not to him and not to their son or daughter who would want to know their father.

She would have to tell him, try to work out some amicable arrangement about the future. Hopefully he would care about what was in the best interests of the child enough to put their differences aside and deal with what was important. She certainly would. This was never going to be the ideal parenting situation for either of them, but with some reasonable co-operation, maybe they could give their child the best of both worlds.

Her hand moved automatically to the top drawer of the desk, opening it and taking out the business card Peter had given her in the park—the card which had made Thomas Harper's mother realise that her selfish possessiveness was not going to go unchallenged. She'd thrown it back on Sarah's desk, not wanting any part of Peter Ramsey, and Erin had picked it up and kept it, secretly wanting every part of the prince she imagined him to be.

She fingered it now, remembering how confident Peter had been in the intimidating power it carried—the might of his wealth behind it. Would he use that power against her?

Her mind churned through a mess of dark, miserable thoughts. Telling him could wait a while, she finally decided. Her most immediate aim was to start looking after herself—and the baby—by eating properly, which might help her sleep better. Some exercise wouldn't go astray, either. A walk along the beach to the shopping centre would do her good. And she needed to buy a book on pregnancy, learn what she should be doing, what was best for the baby.

Yes, that came first.

CHAPTER TEN

Seven months later...

ERIN checked that she had everything ready for the meeting; jug of iced water in the refrigerator, glasses ready on the kitchen bench, coffee percolator loaded—Jane Emerson, her agent, never drank anything else—Earl Grey tea for Richard Long, her very English editor, and a plate of assorted cookies that should please everyone. The living room was tidy, the curtains pulled back to showcase the view of Byron Bay—white sand and crystal clear turquoise water.

She had bought this beach house four years ago. It suited her, right away from the bustle of major cities, especially for writing. She didn't care if the animated film people thought she was some prima donna author, insisting that they travel to her for the consultation on how her story was to be brought to the big screen. At eight months' pregnant, and determined on keeping that fact as private as possible, she didn't want any fanfare about this meeting.

The publicity could come afterwards, when everything had been signed. No doubt her editor and agent would make the most of it, eager to push more book sales on the back of a film created by Zack Freeman who also happened to be an Australian, and top of the tree at delivering the best computerised special effects. He'd won two academy awards for his work. Apparently he was now putting his creativity into animated movies. Erin was looking forward to meeting him, wondering what he planned to do with her story.

The sound of cars pulling up in the street

outside drew her down the hallway to the front door. A glance at her watch assured her it was time for her visitors to arrive, just a couple of minutes short of ten o'clock. They were all staying at the plush Bay Resort on Johnson Street and had probably already established an acquaintance, either last night or this morning. She took a deep breath, mentally put on her author hat, tried to forget how ungainly she looked with her hugely swollen belly, and opened the door.

Richard and Jane were alighting from the first car, a local taxi. Jane was dressed in her London black business suit even though it was November here in Australia, and so hot today at Byron Bay, Erin had dressed comfortably in a sleeveless cotton shift. However, she had the air-conditioning on so Jane shouldn't suffer too much inside the house. Richard was in a suit, too, a grey pinstripe, very English.

Her gaze shifted to the second car, a white

Mercedes. A tall, black-haired man, dressed in a lightweight grey suit, emerged from the front passenger seat. An even taller man, with dark blond hair and very broad shoulders underneath a tailored navy jacket, appeared from the driver's side. He turned towards the house and Erin reeled back in shock.

Peter Ramsey!

Disbelief fought with unmistakable recognition. A tumult of emotions roared through her, putting knots in her stomach, squeezing her heart, shattering her mind. All throughout her pregnancy she'd struggled with facing him about his unplanned fatherhood, and now he was here, about to see what a short weekend of intimacy with her had wrought. He'd hate her for it, accuse her of all sorts of nasty things…

No-o-o-o-o-o….

The scream inside her head pushed her feet into spinning around, moving out of sight. Sheer panic pelted her down the hallway, the need to hide, to avoid this meeting at all costs churning through her. She was breathless, heaving in agitation as she stopped at the sliding glass doors at the far end of the living room, gripping the handles to yank them apart. Pain speared across her lower back.

This frantic activity was not good for her, not good for the baby. She leant her forehead against the glass, willing her insides to calm down. Enough reason filtered through the chaos in her mind to tell her it was madness to run anyway. They'd search for her if she was missing. This was an important business meeting. Millions of dollars were on the line. Richard and Jane had flown out from England for it. Escape simply wasn't possible.

"Erin?"

Jane calling out for her.

She'd left the front door open.

No escape.

Her ears picked up some subdued chat

between her visitors out on porch. Another call came, this time from Richard.

"Erin, are you there?"

She forced herself to answer. "Yes. Come on through."

The pain was receding though it took an act of will to release the door handles and stand up straight. Jane was ushering the men into the living-room, talking brightly, diplomatically covering for their hostess's lack of courtesy in not greeting them properly at the door. They had to be faced now. She took a deep breath, squared her shoulders and turned around.

Jane and Richard were a blur. So was Zack Freeman. Her eyes instantly focused on the father of her child, skating up from grey trousers, white shirt, navy and red striped silk tie, determined chin, no smile on his mouth, strong nose, riveting blue gaze which dropped from her face to the unmistakable evidence of full-blown pregnancy. His whole face tightened into grim shock.

"Erin, this is Zack Freeman who will be the creative director of the film," Jane prattled in cheery introduction. "And Peter Ramsey who'll be underwriting the cost of production. Erin Lavelle, gentlemen."

The black-haired man was moving forward, offering his hand.

Erin stood rooted to the spot, stunned by the fact that Peter was behind this movie project. He knew who she was. He knew only too intimately who she was. He'd hauled his gaze up from her belly and his eyes were like icy steel, stabbing into hers.

"Back off, Zack!" he commanded in a voice that cracked like a whip, stopping the other man in his tracks. "This meeting is adjourned until further notice."

"What?"

"Why?"

"But…"

He waved a sharply dismissive hand at the

flurry of shocked protests. "Go back to the hotel and wait." He dug in his trouser pocket, drew out a set of keys and held them out to his business associate. "Take them in my car, Zack."

His gaze had not so much as flickered from Erin yet he emanated so much intimidating power, no-one was inclined to fight his edict. Besides which, he was the money man, and the flow of tension between her and the big billionaire undoubtedly telegraphed there was a huge hitch in this morning's plan.

Richard was brave enough to ask, "Is it okay to leave you, Erin?"

"Yes. Go," she croaked out, resigned to the inevitable confrontation.

They left.

Peter didn't move.

Neither did she.

After a long nerve-tearing silence, he said, "It's mine, isn't it?"

No doubt in his voice. No doubt in his eyes.

Just wanting the fact confirmed by her, forcing the admission with ruthless determination.

"Yes," she acknowledged.

His mouth twisted in bitter irony. "So your fling with me had a purpose. Should I feel flattered that you chose my genes for your child?"

Her mind boggled over the assumption that her pregnancy had been planned, that she'd used him as a stud. "It was an accident! An accident!" she cried, appalled that he could think she would choose single parenthood after all she'd said on the issue.

He threw up his hands in contempt. "How big a fool do you think I am, Erin? You kept your identity a secret. You lied about contraception…"

"I did not lie about taking the pill!" she hurled back at him. "You can ask my doctor why it didn't work because I don't know. I was still taking it when I went to him five weeks after we parted."

"Five weeks!" he mocked. "You've had a lot of time since then to let me know about this accident. Why did you keep it to yourself?"

"Because…" Her mind whirled around the reasons that had stopped her from making contact with him.

"Because…" he prompted with an air of relentless purpose.

"I didn't need your…your financial support," she blurted out.

Anger blazed from him. "Being independently wealthy does not give you the right to keep me in ignorance of my own flesh and blood."

"I was going to tell you, Peter," she pleaded.

"When?" he bored in.

"After the baby was born. When it was a real child."

"A real child?" His voice rose in incredulity. His gaze targeted her baby bump. "You don't think that's real?"

"There have been complications," she rushed

out, trying to explain what she meant. "I almost had a miscarriage. I was in bed for weeks, trying to keep the baby safe. Then I still wasn't well. The doctor diagnosed gestational diabetes so I've had to be very careful about my diet. It didn't seem…necessary to tell you until—" her hands flapped in wild appeal for his understanding "—until the baby was born alive and well."

"Necessary…" He turned the word into a savage indictment of her decision to leave him out of her pregnancy. "Who looked after you when you needed looking after? Didn't it ever occur to you that *I* might want to provide every care to ensure that my child is safely born?"

No, it hadn't. She'd had no experience of men *caring* to that degree. It was women who did the looking after. But maybe he meant doing what she'd done herself. "I hired a private nurse when I needed help."

"So you shared with a stranger what you

should have shared with me," he slung at her in disgust.

Erin stared at him helplessly, unable to offer any further defence for her decisions. She simply hadn't realised he would care so much about a baby who was yet to be born, that he would feel so *responsible* when she had assured him they were having safe sex. "I was going to tell you, Peter," she said limply, despairing that he would believe anything she said.

"Were you?" His eyes glittered with biting cynicism. "If I hadn't set up this movie deal and kept my name out of it until we met face-to-face, you could have gone on keeping me in ignorance of my child as long as you liked."

There was no use denying it. He wasn't going to accept her word for anything. "Why did you?" she asked, needing some respite from being *the accused,* grabbing at the fact that he'd given no explanation of his actions.

"Why did I what?" he snapped, still in a towering rage over what she'd done.

"Set up this movie deal."

He snorted derisively. "Oh, I had this brilliant idea that if I manipulated you into a situation where you had to sit down and talk to me, we might recapture the click we had when we were just *a man and a woman.*"

The acid sting of those last words—words she'd used to him—brought a rush of hot blood to her face, scorching her cheeks.

"Is that guilt making you blush, Erin?" he mocked. "Was that another lie to gloss over the deception about your identity?"

He was so cold, so relentless in his attack on her integrity. All she could do was shake her head.

He shook his, too, self-mockingly, reminding her of the lengths he'd gone to in order to connect with her again. It made no sense. He hadn't liked her being an author who was more newsworthy than himself. Had her rejection of him rankled? Maybe no woman had ever walked out on Peter Ramsey. Was this an ego thing? Had he thought he could force her into accepting him again? On *his* terms, whatever they were?

"You're very good at manipulating…" The way he'd worked the situation in the park with Dave Harper so he could draw her into meeting him. "Is this some dummy deal, designed solely to get at me, Peter?"

"No, it's absolutely genuine. I wouldn't involve other people in a dummy deal," he shot back, resenting her attack on *his* integrity.

"Did you think your money, your power to make this happen, would make some difference to me?"

"After you refused to be *my doll?*" He rolled his eyes in contempt of her interpretation of his motives. "I'm not a complete idiot, Erin."

"I don't understand where you're coming from," she cried. Why would he set out to increase her fame as an author with a movie of one of her stories if he wanted to pursue a relationship with her? It would put the spotlight on Erin Lavelle wherever they went together.

"That is now totally irrelevant," he said tersely. "There's only one thing you need to understand, Erin."

He walked towards her, aggressive purpose radiating from him, making her heart flutter with fear. This was the warrior unleashed, every atom of his being geared to fight. *Against her.*

A shaft of pain across her lower back increased the tension that was probably causing it. She fought the urge to double up and nurse it through. Pride forced her to stand upright, though she could not control the tremor that ran down her legs as Peter stopped directly in front of her, his big, powerful physique making her feel hopelessly weak.

His eyes burned into hers. He reached out

and very deliberately spread a hand over her baby bulge, making her skin burn under the heat of its possessive claim. "You will not shut me out of my child's life any longer," he said, the hard edge of ruthlessness in his voice telling her she had no choice.

She couldn't fight him. Didn't really want to. He did have the right to know his child. But she couldn't bear him thinking she'd meant to shut him out. It wasn't true. She wouldn't have done that. Yet how could she make him believe her?

Her whirling mind clutched at a little piece of evidence. "I was going to tell you, Peter. I'll show you," she threw at him, quickly sidestepping, sliding away from his touch, mentally pumping strength back into her legs as she charged across the living-room to the door leading to her study.

"Show me what?"

She ignored the question. He was hard on her heels, anyway. Seeing is believing, she thought wildly, flinging the study door open wide for him to follow and heading straight for her writing desk.

"Good God! Was *this* what you were thinking of when you were watching the races at Randwick?"

He had to be looking at the paintings of the winged horses, commissioned from the artist who illustrated her books. They were hanging on the study wall—inspiration while she'd been writing the story. "Yes. *The Mythical Horses of Mirrima*," she answered distractedly. "You should have waited for that one if you want to make a movie of one of my books. It's the best I've done."

"You wrote a story while you were so concerned about your pregnancy?"

The harshly critical tone in his voice implied she'd lied about having complications, as well as everything else.

"Thinking up words is not exactly physical

labour," she retorted, flashing him a resentful look as she rounded the desk. "And it kept my mind off other things."

"Like a nagging conscience over hiding my child from me?"

"I wasn't going to!" she almost shouted at him.

He'd stopped just inside the study and cut a terribly forbidding figure, making her quail at trying to convince him of anything. But she had to. A future of gut-wrenching conflict between them had to be averted.

"Look!" she cried, pulling out the top drawer of her desk and grabbing the business card she'd fingered so many times, agonising over calling him, holding it out for him to see. "I kept it. Why would I have it so handy if I never meant to contact you?"

The laser blue eyes were briefly hooded as his gaze dropped to the card that was being shakily offered to him. For several nerve-wracking seconds he stared at it. His face remained grim. Her challenge wasn't working. She wasn't reaching him.

"For God's sake, Peter! You told me how you'd feel about your own children. How could I not give you the chance to be a hands-on father?"

It drew his gaze up to hers again, not quite so bitterly condemning now but still sceptical of her intentions.

"Remember our conversation about the Harpers?" she begged in appeal.

"I remember you saying you would only have a child within the security of a truly committed marriage," he bit out as though that was another lie.

Anguish twisted through her, spilling into pleading words. "Doesn't that tell you this pregnancy was an accident? I didn't use you. I didn't plan anything. I've just been trying to get on with my own life until…"

Pain…more savage than before. She gasped, instinctively bending over to contain it.

"Erin?"

She couldn't answer the sharp inquiry. Her mind was yelling at her to breathe in quick pants, relax, ease the agony. Then to her horror, a gush of water drenched her panties and ran down her legs.

"Oh, no…no…" she wailed.

"What's wrong?"

She lifted her head.

Peter was striding towards her, full of urgent concern now.

"The baby," she cried. "The baby is coming."

CHAPTER ELEVEN

A COMPLETELY different fear gripped Erin as Peter gently lowered her into the chair she used for writing—fear for the baby. Something had to be wrong for it to be coming a month early. She wrapped her arms protectively around her belly, rocking it in an agony of hope that all was still well.

"Try to stay calm. Panic won't help," Peter coolly advised. "Give me your doctor's name and I'll get things moving for you."

"Davis." She nodded to the telephone on the desk. "Press six for his surgery."

Within seconds he was acting for her. "This is Peter Ramsey, calling on behalf of Erin

Lavelle. I need to be connected to Dr Davis immediately. This is an emergency."

A waiting pause, then, "Yes, I am that Peter Ramsey. I'm with Erin Lavelle. Her water has broken and she's suffering labour pain. I'd appreciate it if you'd despatch an ambulance immediately to her house on Ocean Drive, number 14, and meet us at the hospital when we get there."

Another pause.

The bad pain had receded, leaving only a dull ache. Erin couldn't help wondering how Dr Davis was reacting to a string of demands, backed by the power of the Ramsey name and everything it stood for.

"Thank you," Peter said, obviously having received a satisfactory reply. He put the telephone receiver back in its cradle and turned his attention to her, catching the frown of concern on her face. "I've missed something?" he asked.

"You're going to turn this birth into a three-ring-circus bandying your name about like that."

His eyes glittered derisively at her complaint. "You might as well start getting used to it, Erin. You'll be attached to the Ramsey zoo for a long time to come. And quite frankly, I don't give a damn for your reclusive inclinations in this particular instance. For the sake of our child, I'm asking for top priority service, and since my mother has guided my father into donating millions to the medical system of this country, I consider it a reasonable request."

It probably was. And she was grateful that he had ensured quick attention for her and the baby, grateful that he was here, helping her. "I'm sorry. It just seemed…unnecessary. I'm not…not thinking straight."

"Don't worry about it," he said more kindly. "Just let me take care of everything. Do you want to get out of these wet clothes while we're waiting for the ambulance or do you think it's best not to move?"

"I'm frightened of moving."

"Okay. I'll have the ambulance people bring in a stretcher."

"There's a bag packed ready for going into hospital. It's in my bedroom, along the hallway on the right."

"I'll put it by the front door. Is it all right for me to leave you for a minute?"

"Yes."

But the moment he left the study the pain cut through her again. She struggled out of the chair and leaned against the desk. Somehow that was easier for her to manage the contraction than from a seated position. Peter came back, stood beside her, stroked her hair, making her choke up at the unexpected gesture of tender caring from him.

"Won't be long before the ambulance arrives," he murmured sympathetically.

Tears swam into her eyes. She couldn't speak. It ran through her mind that if she *had* told him about her pregnancy, maybe he would have looked after her. Independence was all very well—she had coped—but it had been very lonely and she was intensely relieved not to be alone right now, to have Peter taking charge of everything.

He remained by her side; in the ambulance, at the hospital, in the labour ward. No one questioned his right to be there. The nurses seemed to regard him with awe, quickly answering anything he wanted to know. Dr Davis also treated him with considerable deference as he monitored Erin's labour, assuring them both that everything was proceeding normally.

It never once occurred to Erin to protest his presence. Although he hadn't declared himself the father of her child to all and sundry, there was no denying he was, and she wanted him with her at the birth. However deep their differences, they had made this baby together and it felt right for their child to be welcomed into the world by both parents.

The contractions were coming fast. She barely had time to catch her breath in between the waves of pain. Peter sat beside her, watching anxiously, giving her his hand to grip, repeating what the doctor said—*head engaged, won't be long, bearing down soon*—as though she couldn't hear for herself, or he needed to assure himself that this agony had a short time limit.

Erin didn't try to speak. She'd stipulated a natural childbirth, thinking she might never have another child and wanting to remember everything about having this one. Her entire concentration was focussed on willing her baby to make a safe journey from her womb, imagining every pain as a positive step forward. The urge to push came suddenly and was almost uncontrollable.

"Not too hard, Erin," the doctor instructed. "Slow it down if you can, a nice, gentle passage, no tearing. Yes, that's good…coming now…head in my hands…"

She felt a rush of release, heard her baby cry, and tears welled into her eyes.

"It's over…over," Peter murmured huskily, gently wiping the trickle of moisture spilling down her cheeks.

"You have a healthy baby boy," the doctor declared. "And despite being a month early, he's a good birth weight, Erin. Nothing for you to worry about."

The assurance brought a further gush of tears. She'd worried so much about so many things, but now her baby was safely born and she didn't have to let Peter Ramsey know he was a father because he was right here, and he couldn't be angry with her for giving him a son, could he? There was no anger at all in the caring way he was mopping up her emotional spillover, trying to calm her down with soothing words.

"It's okay, Erin. You did it. And the baby's fine. I'll bring him to you."

He rose from his chair. She realised he must have been anxious about the birth, too, worrying over having brought on premature labour by raging over her decisions. He probably felt the same overwhelming relief she did. It would be silly to read too much into his caring for her. She was the mother of his child—reason enough to set other issues aside for a more appropriate time.

"Cord clamped. All wrapped up ready to go," Dr Davis said cheerfully, laying their newborn son in the crook of Peter's arm. "We'll just clean up here, then leave the three of you together."

Three...

Linked for the rest of our lives, Erin thought, watching Peter's face as he looked down at the baby who would be part of his future. How large a part would Peter want? A whimsical little smile tugged at the corners of his mouth as he murmured in a bemused tone, "He's so little."

You're so big.

"Won't be when he grows up," Dr Davis remarked knowingly. "He's a long baby. Going to be a tall boy."

Peter's smile widened into a grin. *Just like me,* was written all over it. Would the likeness make his paternal possessiveness stronger? Fear fluttered through Erin's heart. What if he fought her for more than his fair share of their child? She held out her arms, wanting to hug her baby to herself.

The grin remained, Peter's vivid blue eyes sparkling with warm delight as he obliged her, carefully laying their son on her chest, snuggling him between her breasts. It felt so good to hold him at last, not a bump anymore, but a wonderful little person who was snuffling towards one breast as though he could already smell his mother's milk.

A smile broke out on her own face as a surge of love rose above every other emotion, momentarily blotting out the conflict that his life would inevitably bring between her and Peter. Despite the problems of her pregnancy, she'd given safe birth to this miraculous little being…her baby, her very own child.

Peter sat down again, reached out and ran a featherlight finger over the fuzz of fine hair, sounding immensely pleased as he commented, "He's fair. Charlotte's son has very dark hair like Damien's."

Not like a Ramsey. But this son was. That was what he was thinking.

Erin took a deep breath, fighting the fear that frayed her nerves. "Baby hair often falls out, Peter," she said as calmly as she could. "There's no telling what colouring he'll have further down the track."

"Whatever…"

Not the slightest crack in his good humour.

Erin heaved a sigh of relief. Maybe she was fearful of too much and Peter would not try to take the lion's share of their child. Right now he was exuding pleasure. She should relax, enjoy the maternal rush of holding her baby.

Dr Davis finished clearing up, assured Erin that the afterbirth procedure had gone well—no problems at all—had a few words with Peter, informing him that Erin and the baby would soon be moved to a private room where their every comfort and need would be looked after. The latter exchange reminded her that respect for the Ramsey name had ensured every care had been taken and would be taken, and she should be appreciative of the fact.

She looked at the wall clock as the doctor and nurse moved out, closing the door behind them. It surprised her to see it was only just past one o'clock—a relatively quick birth, though the labour had seemed to go on for a long, long time. She looked directly at Peter who had resumed his seat at her bedside.

"Thank you for all you've done."

There was a flash of irony in his eyes. "The least I could do in the circumstances."

For a moment she forgot the indomitable warrior who would fight for what he wanted, and remembered the prince, riding in to the rescue—the magnificent man he had been in her imagination. "I'm glad you were here for me. For us," she said huskily.

"I would have been all along if you'd let me, Erin," he replied, restirring her guilt for not telling him about her pregnancy.

"I'm sorry."

He shook his head. "It's gone." The blue eyes pierced hers with determined purpose. "We're here now. And we have our son to consider."

"Yes," she agreed, though her mind instantly shied away from discussing the future. Her hand curled protectively around her baby's head as she turned her gaze from Peter and looked at their son, not wanting him torn between two worlds.

"Have you thought of any names for him?"

They were not fighting words. There was a smile in his voice. Erin's inner tension eased a little. Peter wouldn't want their son hurt by a conflict between his mother and father. Surely he'd do his utmost to prevent it.

"I like Jack," she answered.

"Jack…Jack Ramsey. Sounds good. I like it, too."

Erin's jaw tightened. She had to stop this take-over, stand up for her rights. Her eyes flashed her own determination. "It will be Jack Lavelle."

The soft indulgence instantly disappeared from his face, replaced by a steely resolution that wasn't about to brook any opposition. "You said the pregnancy was an accident, Erin," he reminded her. "Was that the truth?"

"Yes," she replied unflinchingly.

"Were you speaking the truth when you told me you would only bring a child into this world within the emotional security of a fully committed marriage?"

"Yes. But this was unplanned, Peter. I'm only too aware that it's not the ideal situation I talked about. I can't help that. I hope—"

"Yes, you can," he cut in, his eyes boring into hers. "You can help our son to have all he should have from his mother and father."

"I'll do my best to come to a fair agreement with you."

"How good is your best?" he challenged. "Will you go so far as to pledge yourself to a fully committed marriage with me?"

The totally unexpected proposal stunned her into silence. She stared at him, feeling the mental pressure he was applying, realising he already had his mind set on what course should be taken and was ruthlessly intent on making it happen.

Marriage…to Peter Ramsey!

Words he'd spoken to her earlier bounced around her dazed mind… *You'll be attached to the Ramsey zoo for a long time to come. Might as well start getting used to it.*

It was ridiculously old-fashioned to get married for the sake of a child. People didn't do it these days. There was no need to, particularly in this country. If unmarried mothers were in economic difficulties, they could get child support from the government. Besides, Peter knew she was independently wealthy. No financial problems. But he wasn't talking financial support. He was targeting emotional security for their son, having both parents form a tight family unit for him.

"You can't *want* to marry me," she cried, seizing on the hard reality that unresolvable issues between parents did not provide a happy home life for a child.

"Why not?" he shot back, unmoved by her protest.

"You keep accusing me of lying, Peter. When there's such a big trust problem between us…it would wear us both down, you suspecting me of God knows what, me having to defend everything I do or say. It would be a hell of a relationship. Bad for our child, not good."

"If you could learn to be more open with me," he retorted pointedly, "we wouldn't have a problem, would we? It's silence that breeds a lack of trust—hiding things that shouldn't be hidden. Be straight with me, Erin. It's as simple as that."

She remembered Alicia Hemmings calling him a strait-laced bastard. Perhaps she should have taken more heed of that warning. There was no denying she had been at fault, not telling him she'd fallen pregnant, not correcting his assumption that she was a preschool teacher, which, of course, was at the heart of her biggest problem with him. *The author* thing invariably messed with men's minds, making them resentful of her success and the celebrity that went with it.

"It's not so simple, Peter," she said dispiritedly.

"Yes, it is," he insisted. "And you can't say we're not sexually compatible. I'd count that as a huge plus for our marriage."

Was that why he'd come after her with this movie deal…remembering the incredibly erotic and passionate sex they'd had together, wanting it again? She searched his eyes, saw only a burning conviction that he was right and she couldn't refute the argument. Yet how long would great sex last when he began resenting what she did and the attention it drew to her?

"Can you really see yourself living happily with what I am—a writer whose imagination can be triggered at any time, losing my awareness of you and your needs?"

"I'd never try to stop you from doing your thing, Erin," he asserted, without even pausing to consider the situation. "You have a unique talent and I'd consider it a crime to put any limitation on it. We'll hire a nanny in case you forget to feed Jack or—"

"I'm not that bad," she cut in sharply. An adult who could look after himself was one thing, her own child quite another. "There's no way I'd neglect Jack."

"Whatever. It's best he has me to give him attention when your mind is drifting elsewhere. That's how a partnership works," he said with satisfaction, apparently not the least bit perturbed about her need for time and space.

But he hadn't lived with it, hadn't been irritated and frustrated by it. He'd only experienced one short episode of it at Randwick and that had been more of a curiosity because it hadn't happened to him before.

"What about when publicity centres on me instead of you?" she mocked, not believing he would be so reasonable about that knock to his ego.

He frowned as though he didn't understand what she was getting at. "You can have as much or as little publicity as you like. Though I'd have to say you're bound to get more when we're married. Unavoidable. I can and will protect you from the worst of it, but any time we appear in public together..."

"Oh, come on!" she cried, exasperated by his dismissal of the point. "You don't like me taking the spotlight from you. Every man I've been close to has resented it after a while and you're no exception, Peter Ramsey. It instantly stuck in your craw that a newspaper headline was more about me than you."

"It stuck in my craw that you'd deliberately deceived me about who you were," he retorted fiercely. "I wouldn't care if I never made another headline. It sure as hell doesn't do anything for me."

His vehemence rattled her judgement of the situation. Had she completely misread his reaction to the newspaper story? Feeling hope-lessly confused, she held her tongue, needing time to review what had happened between them, try to see it from his point of view.

"I'm sorry. I shouldn't have raised my voice," he muttered, throwing a glance of concern at their baby who was making a mewing sound, wrinkling up his little face, maybe sensing the tension in the room and not liking it.

"It's okay," Erin crooned, softly stroking her tiny son's cheek. "Mummy loves you."

"So does Daddy." The words were spoken very quietly but they were undoubtedly a fighting declaration from Peter. He wasn't about to be sidelined from their lives.

Jack sighed and rested contentedly again.

"He is my son and heir," Peter stated, his eyes biting in their intensity. "He can't be brought up in an unprotected environment, Erin. You will find life much easier within the

Ramsey fold. In fact, it's the only way to give Jack security in every sense."

The heir to billions…her thinking had not encompassed what that might mean to their child. Peter had lived with it all his life. He knew.

"No one has to know," she said impulsively. "If he's Jack Lavelle…"

"I will not hide my son's existence," he grated out.

"He might be more protected that way, have a chance of a normal life," she pleaded.

"Don't even imagine for one moment that I will not lay claim to him."

He was right. She couldn't imagine it. That was not the kind of man he was. The sense of a trap closing around her—a trap where she had no control over anything—was very strong. The power of the Ramsey name suddenly reminded her of how she'd become connected to Peter in the first place—the little boy, Thomas, separated from his father, the issue of custody.

"What happened with Dave Harper?"

"That has nothing to do with us," came the curt dismissal.

"I want to know."

Her insistence caused his jaw to tighten. He didn't want to go down that road, but she kept her gaze locked on his, determined on an answer.

"It's not relevant to our situation, Erin," he grated out.

"I want to know," she repeated, refusing to be closed off on this point which somehow seemed very relevant to her.

"Right!" he snapped. "I placed Dave Harper in a position where he could sell on commission, choosing his own hours to work so he could look after his son without help. Given the lies his wife had told about him, and the fact that she had placed Thomas in daily care at a preschool and had a nanny to look after him the rest of the time, leaving her free to carry on a very social life with her new partner, the family court decided the father would be the better nurturing parent and awarded him major custody."

Major custody...lies told...

The trap closing around her felt even tighter, the fear growing that she could lose her child to Peter—her one and only child.

A knock on the door was a welcome interruption. Erin felt stressed and exhausted. A matronly nurse entered the room, accompanied by two male hospital orderlies.

"We're here to wheel you to your own room, Miss Lavelle. Get you and your baby settled there," the nurse announced, smiling brightly at both her and Peter. "And I think I should inform you, Mr Ramsey, that news has got out about your being here with Miss Lavelle. Hospital Reception has been fending off inquiries. Perhaps you'd be good enough to deal with the disturbance, settle the interest that's apparently been stirred?"

Peter heaved a vexed sigh and rose to his full formidable height, clearly girding himself to face a different battle. "How good is security in the maternity wing?" he asked the nurse.

"No unauthorised person will get past my station, Mr Ramsey," she confidently assured him. "Miss Lavelle should rest now and I shall see to it that she does."

"Thank you." He took Erin's hand and gave it a light squeeze to command her attention. "The three ring circus is about to begin," he said mockingly. "And I'm perfectly happy for you to be the star of this show, Erin."

"I don't want to be, Peter," she cried, panicking at the thought of being hounded by the media.

"It's inescapable."

"You don't have to tell anybody anything," she pleaded.

"That would only make the problem worse. They'd keep digging."

"What will you tell them?"

"The truth. The one really good thing about the truth is it doesn't come back and bite you. Keeping secrets is what messes everything up." He paused to let this all too relevant truth sink home. Then totally careless of the fact that other people were listening, he bored in with, "Do I have your consent to announcing that we're getting married in the near future?"

Inescapable...

She *was* trapped.

Her mind whirled, trying to grasp some other workable way to handle the future. The identity of her own child made going it alone a nightmare of complications. Besides which, Peter wouldn't leave them alone. She was locked into this relationship for the rest of their lives. And if she had to fight him for custody...

Maybe marriage was the best course to take. She could try it.

Peter couldn't force her to stay married to him if it turned into a miserable disaster.

"It's the right thing to do, Erin."

She looked up to a blaze of conviction in the steely-blue eyes.

"Yes." The word spilled from her lips, the sense of inevitability too overwhelming to fight.

He nodded his satisfaction. "Rest easy now. I'll go and fix everything that has to be fixed." He leaned over and kissed their son's forehead, murmuring. "Be good for your mother."

With one last searing look at Erin, a look that burned its message into her brain—*We are committed and there's no turning back*—he headed for the door—a big man with broad shoulders, strong enough to handle anything he was faced with.

A whisper of hope drifted through the anxious chaos in Erin's mind. Maybe Peter Ramsey was her prince after all. She took comfort in that thought. It was the only comfort to be had at this point in time.

The die was cast.

They were going to be married.

And she desperately wanted to believe they could live happily ever after.

CHAPTER TWELVE

Two months…two months of holding himself in check while Erin recovered from Jack's birth and made the adjustment from her solitary life to what it meant to be a Ramsey. The waiting was almost over. Tonight she would be his wife. She would share his bed and the desire that had driven him to set up a second meeting with her could finally be freed from the constrictions he'd placed upon it.

The wedding had to come first.

He'd taken every care not to give Erin any cause to change her mind about their marriage, always keeping their son's welfare as the prime reason for it. The sex, which had been so memorable to him and had to be to her, as well, was a secondary lure, promising that the commitment would not be without pleasure. However, the fact that she'd walked away from it once had made him wary of using it as a form of pressure to keep her on track. Once the marriage vows were taken, there would be no walking away.

Ever again.

Which was precisely how he wanted it.

"You're looking grim, Peter. Is everything okay between you and Erin?"

He finished fastening the second cuff link and lifted his gaze to Damien who was standing by, holding the buttonhole carnation ready to be attached to his lapel. He'd been best man for Damien Wynter at his wedding to Charlotte and his friend was now returning the favour.

"Have you detected anything wrong?" he asked, aware of how astute Damien was. He and Charlotte had spent quite a lot of time with

Erin since they'd arrived from London for Christmas, staying on for the wedding. They liked her and he thought she liked them, especially warming to his sister, perhaps even confiding some anxiety about the future.

"No. Just aware that you're rather tense," was the dry response.

It drew a wry smile from Peter. "I've manipulated Erin into this marriage, just as you did with Charlotte. I'm hoping it works out as well as yours has."

"I hope so, too. She's a very special woman." No criticism from Damien. Sympathetic understanding in his dark eyes. "You did what you had to do, Peter. Don't fret it. Just go on and win. I have every confidence that you'll find a way to Erin's heart. If you haven't already."

"What makes you say that?"

"Making a movie of *The Mythical Horses of Mirrima* is a masterstroke. Shows you listened to her. Shows you appreciate her wonderfully creative story-telling. Shows you're not jealous of her career as a writer because you're giving it a boost. And having Zack Freeman consult with her over the screenplay shows respect for her right to have her own vision transferred to a different medium."

Which all demonstrated to Peter just how astute Damien was. "Read me like a book," he conceded, reaching for the buttonhole to pin it on.

"You're a master tactician. I've always admired that in you."

But what his head told him was one thing, what he felt with Erin Lavelle was quite another. He wanted her to respond to him as she had before. He needed that from her. Having his son wasn't enough.

The white carnation was the final touch, marking him as the groom. He wondered what his bride was thinking, feeling. She was in the other wing of the family mansion, having been his mother's guest here at Palm Beach ever since they'd left Byron Bay and come to Sydney. Charlotte was with her now, carrying out the role of matron of honour.

Had Erin been watching the limousines roll in, bringing the wedding guests to the huge marquee in the grounds, thinking how few of them had been invited by her? This wedding was *his* show. But it was for her, to give her the spotlight as his bride, to give her all she deserved to have. Her own parents would not have provided it. They'd been only too happy for Peter to take it on. Even her mother who had remarried a few years ago. It was only too obvious her second husband came first, her daughter an almost unwelcome reminder that she had been married before.

Erin had been out of any family life for a long time. Alone in a way he'd never been alone. At least she had his family now. And Jack. Her love for their son was a beautiful thing to see. This marriage would work. He'd make it work.

"You're getting that grim face again, Peter," Damien warned.

He forced himself to relax. "I was just thinking it might have been easier for Erin to get married in a registry office as she suggested, instead of all this pomp and ceremony."

"No." A very decisive no. "I have it on good authority—namely my wife—that every woman wants a wedding to remember and a no frills affair does not meet the mark." He clamped a hand on Peter's shoulder. "Time for us to get going. Let's make it a happy night."

"Right! Thanks for your support, Damien."

"My pleasure."

They grinned at each other—both of them born warriors who would not accept defeat. They would stand shoulder to shoulder at this wedding and if happiness could be won, they would win it.

* * *

"Here!" Charlotte handed her the bridal bouquet and stood back to eye the full effect of how Erin would appear, walking down the aisle. "Perfect!" she declared. "Your fans are going to love the photos. You look just like a fairy-tale princess bride."

Erin stared at her reflection in the cheval mirror, her heart lifting at seeing herself precisely how she had dreamt of looking as a bride. She loved the sweetheart neckline of her dress—old-fashioned perhaps, but the more modern strapless dresses had not been what she had envisioned for herself.

The tightly moulded bodice was beautifully beaded with tiny crystals, as was the hem and lower half of the gloriously wide skirt. A diamond tiara—lent to her by Peter's mother—held the veil which frothed out to form a magical frame for her long black hair, softly curling down over her shoulders. A make-up artist had done wonders with her face. It could be called beautiful today. It really could.

She was glad now that Peter had pushed her into accepting a big, formal wedding. He'd been right to do it. Right about so many things. His family had welcomed her into its fold, making meeting them, being with them, incredibly easy. Christmas had been marvellous, especially with Charlotte and Damien being here with their two-year-old son, James, and their four-month-old daughter, Genevieve. The warmth, the laughter, the gift-giving…it had felt so good to be part of it. Not an outsider at all.

Even Lloyd Ramsey, who looked so terribly intimidating, had turned out to be surprisingly charming. And he loved Jack. His new grandson was definitely the apple of his eye. He'd perch Jack on his big, broad chest while he read the newspaper, informing the baby of any interesting movement on the share market.

"This boy is a Ramsey," he'd declared. "Can't start learning too soon."

The past two months had been a huge learning curve for Erin. She'd been very wrong about Peter's mother viewing her as an interesting curiosity. Kate truly admired her work, knew every story she'd written. And Lloyd Ramsey admired the fact that she was a performer, using her God-given talent to the best of her ability, making a big success of it.

No-one expected her to stop writing and just be Peter's wife. Least of all, Peter, who was determined on increasing public awareness of her authorship with his movie of *The Mythical Horses of Mirrima*.

"Happy?" Charlotte asked, grinning at her.

Erin smiled back. "I couldn't look better. And you look stunning, too."

Charlotte was wearing a gold satin sheath, perfect for her colouring. Her hair was darker than Peter's, more caramel with blond streaks, and she had amber eyes, not blue. To Erin's mind, Charlotte and Damien, who was tall, dark and strikingly handsome, were a golden couple. They shone with happiness in their love for each other. She fiercely hoped this marriage would work, that she and Peter could end up living happily ever after together.

"Something wrong?" Charlotte asked.

Erin shook her mind back to the present. "No. Everything's fine."

"You went away for a moment." There was a frown of concern on her face.

"I have a habit of doing that," Erin quickly replied, grimacing an apology.

The frown didn't clear. "It didn't look like a good place, Erin. Are you okay with marrying Peter?"

"Yes. Yes, I am. He's a good man. I've never met better." That was the absolute truth.

Charlotte's expression turned reflective. "You know, I didn't love Damien when I married him. He more or less rescued me from a nasty situation and I took the chance he offered to turn humiliation into a triumph."

"You're very well matched."

"Yes." A wicked grin burst across her face. "And he's still the sexiest man in the world for me." One eye arched in provocative inquiry. "I take it you were hot for Peter when Jack was conceived?"

"Very much so," she answered wryly.

"Well, I don't know what went wrong between you two back then, but if that primal spark is still there, it sort of pushes you into growing closer together. Just don't hold back on it, Erin. Peter needs to be wanted for himself, you know. Not for what he can give."

"I know." She smiled to show that she understood. "Thank you, Charlotte."

Erin was only too aware of how much Peter was giving. It was an embarrassment of riches all going one way. She wasn't giving him anything except ready access to their son. Although she had given up control of her own life, her independence, and she couldn't help thinking that all Peter's *gifts* were aimed at sweetening her surrender to this marriage.

He wanted Jack.

But she wasn't sure he still wanted her.

He hadn't once tried to reignite the primal spark, not with a look, a kiss…no attempt whatsoever to establish any form of physical intimacy between them. It made Erin worry that, in his mind, she was still tainted by her lies of omission. She felt very nervous about what would happen tonight, when the wedding was over, how it would be as his wife, not just the mother of his child.

"Time for us to get going, Erin," Charlotte said. "Ready?"

"Yes, I'm ready."

Ready to seal the commitment she had made, for better or for worse. From the day of their son's birth, Peter had been driving her towards this moment. There was no turning back. Let it be done now, she thought on a wave of fateful resignation. Deal with what came after…after.

They went downstairs.

Her father was waiting in the grand foyer, ready to escort her to the marquee and give her away. He'd given her away when she was seven, Erin thought. Peter would never do that to Jack.

She had to make this marriage work.

Had to.

A princess…a gut-wrenchingly beautiful princess. Peter's heart started galloping as she walked down the aisle towards him. A surge of desire tightened his groin.

His bride.

The woman he'd wanted more than any other.

But she wasn't smiling.

Her gaze was tightly focused on him, not

even a glance at the guests on either side of red carpet she trod with deliberately measured steps. Her chin was held high. Peter read determination on her face, and he was suddenly riven with doubt.

Had he done right by her in hemming her into this marriage?

Too late to change anything now.

And he didn't want to.

A fierce wave of possessiveness ran through him. Erin…Jack…both of them belonged with him. He would make her see it, make her believe it.

Yet he couldn't get rid of the doubt. It plagued him during the wedding service and throughout the reception afterwards. He put on a happy face. To Erin's credit she put on a happy face, too. They fulfilled the role of a happy couple in front of the sea of guests.

But it was a strain to Peter and he sensed the hidden tension in Erin, too. He was glad when ten o'clock came—the agreed time for Erin to slip away from the party to breast-feed Jack. The festive dinner had been eaten, the speeches were over, the cake had been cut, coffee was being served.

"I'll come with you," he said, keeping his arm hooked around hers as he guided her to the exit of the marquee.

She threw him a startled look. "You don't have to. You have so many friends here, Peter."

"I want to."

He didn't care if she preferred to be alone for a while. She was his bride, his wife, and be damned if he'd lose her, even for a moment, on this, their wedding night.

Her fingers fluttered nervously across his coat-sleeve, but she voiced no further protest. Once they were outside and on the path through the rose garden to the conservatory, he heard her suck in a deep breath as though she was short of oxygen.

"Thank you for the wedding, Peter," she said softly. "Everything's been beautiful."

Mega-wealth could buy everything beautiful, he thought cynically, but it can't buy the heart of a woman. At least he knew Erin hadn't married him for his billions.

"I wanted it to be a fairy-tale wedding for you, Erin," he said with a dash of irony, aware that love should have been at the centre of it. "Fit for the princess in the park," he added, remembering how taken he had been with her on that first day of meeting.

She stopped walking. He halted beside her, seeing the angst on her face as she shook her head, tensing, not knowing what it meant. Then she looked up at him, her beautiful green eyes filled with a vulnerability that squeezed his heart.

"You were my prince that day, Peter. I wish we could go there again. I regret, very much, deciding not to tell you I was the author. I just didn't want to spoil the fantasy. But I ended up spoiling everything. And I'm sorry…sorry…"

A wild hope soared through his mind. "I thought it meant you'd planned only a brief fling with me," he said, trying to explain his reaction to the deception.

"I did."

It was like a punch in the gut.

"I didn't believe that with you being who you are, and me being who I am, the attraction we had could lead to any real future together," she rushed on. "But I wanted so much to have you want me…"

"What about now, Erin?" he couldn't stop himself from asking, his desire for her racing hot through his veins, kicked into uncontrollable acceleration by the admission of the desire she had once felt so strongly for him. "Do you believe in a future for us now?" he pressed.

"You've made it so different to what I had imagined…expected…"

"Good different?"

"Oh, yes! Yes!" she cried so fervently, hope soared again, gathering a sense of triumph in the tactics he'd used to wipe out her fears and doubts.

"I want our marriage to work, Erin."

"So do I," she said with no lessening of fervour.

"Then it will," he said confidently.

He wanted to crush her to him. Only the fact that Jack might have woken up and be yelling with hunger held him back. He hugged her arm, bringing her closer to him as they walked on, their bodies touching, and he burned with the need to have her to himself all the way to the nursery.

The nanny had Jack cradled against her shoulder, patting his back. Erin whipped off her veil, draped it over the cot-rail, unzipped the wedding dress, lifted her arms out of the cap sleeves, let the bodice hang from her waist, unclipped a white lacy bra, removed it, slung it over the veil, moved quickly to the rocking chair—all this with her back turned to him. She picked up a towel which had been laid on the armrest of the chair, arranged it over one shoulder, then sat down, holding out her arms for their son.

The nanny gave him to her and Jack instantly latched onto one bared breast, sucking as though his life depended on it. Which it did, Peter thought, wishing that the bond between him and Erin were so simple. Her face was flushed. Was she embarrassed by his watching her breast-feed their child? He hadn't done it before, careful not to impinge on space and time which she might consider very personal and private.

He dismissed the nanny, saying they'd call her when they were ready to leave, and settled in another chair. Of course, there'd been another reason for staying out of the nursery at feeding time. As he had suspected it would be, he found watching Erin suckling their son almost unbearably erotic, tiny hands kneading her milk-laden breast, the absorption in the physical link between them. It was weird to feel jealous of his son, but he did, probably because it had been so long since he had known such an intimate connection with Erin.

"Is he always this hungry?" he asked, his voice gruff with too many raw emotions.

"Yes." She flicked him a look that seemed oddly desperate.

It disturbed him too much to let it pass. "Is my being here worrying you?"

"No." She shook her head vehemently.

She kept too much to herself. He realised now that it was habitual, ingrained from her childhood, her defence against the emotional upheaval of her parents' broken marriage— her road to self-survival, self-sufficiency—but understanding why it was so did not ease his frustration with it.

"Tell me what you're thinking," he demanded.

She slowly lifted her gaze from Jack, her

eyes a dark green tumultuous sea of uncertainty. She took a deep breath, as though gathering up courage, then blurted out, "Tell me you still want me, Peter. Not because I'm Jack's mother. Me…the person I am. Everything you now know about me."

It stunned him that she was in any doubt. Hadn't all his actions proved how much he wanted her in his life? Yet clearly she was apprehensive about his answer, tending almost frantically to their son, lifting him up to her shoulder, rubbing his back until he burped, then transferring him to her other breast. Only when Jack was resettled did she brave another look at him.

His mouth curved into a self-mocking smile as the strength of his feelings for her tore at his chest. "You asked me once if I was a jealous man. I said I wasn't but I find myself jealous of my own son, wanting to be as close to you as he is."

Another wave of heat scorched her cheeks.

If it was embarrassment, he didn't care.

He was laying out the truth, being straight with her.

"Even after you walked away from me, I couldn't stop wanting you, Erin. My mother said you had to have a beautiful mind to have written the books she'd read. It drove me into buying them, reading all of them. And I agreed with her. It made me want you all the more. I set up the movie deal in the hope that it would win you around to wanting me again."

He heaved a sigh to relieve the tightness in his chest. Her gaze was clinging to his. No anguish in her eyes now. More an urgent intensity, begging for more.

"Then there was Jack. Which completely threw me. You'd so decisively shut me out, even when I had the right to know we'd made a child." He leaned forward, forearms on his knees, hands gesturing futility as he shook his head. "I won't even try to explain what I felt then. I know I shamelessly used Jack to get you, and right then I didn't care if you wanted me or not. I was going to have both of you and I would have done anything to force that end."

"I'm glad you did, Peter," she inserted with startling vehemence.

"Glad that I invaded your life and carried you off?" he queried.

"Yes. I didn't want to be alone. I just didn't know how to…how to fix things between us. I got it all wrong. I know I did. These past two months…everything you've done… I was such a fool for giving you the kind of ego that ended up blighting other relationships I've had. You're not like that at all. The day in the park… I thought you were a big man in every sense, and I should have trusted my instincts. You are. And your family…your family has been a revelation to me. They're interested, they care… I like being part of it."

The relief at hearing her speak her mind and

heart so openly was mountainous. "Then I haven't done wrong by you."

"No." Her eyes glowed with eloquent appeal as a rather tentative, shy little smile softened her face. "You *are* my prince, Peter."

It took an extreme act of will to remain in the chair. Jack was still feeding. He had to hold himself in check for a while yet. But he could spill out what he felt in words.

"Remember that first night out on the balcony of my apartment?"

"Vividly."

The intense emotion in her voice encouraged him to reveal his own. "You wove a spell around me that I can't break, Erin. I want you so badly I can barely sit here and wait for our son to be satisfied. I want to hold you, kiss you, touch you, make mad violent love to you, but I also want to feel the same passionate response that you gave me in the past."

She stared at him, as though caught in a spell

herself. Her lips parted, releasing a rush of breath. Then life returned to her eyes—a brilliant sparkling life, as though a volcano of joy had erupted inside her.

"Press the call-button for the nanny, Peter," she said, detaching Jack from her breast and lifting him to her shoulder.

"He's had enough?"

"Enough for now."

There was no wail of protest from their son and Peter was not about to query Erin's decision. If it meant what he thought it meant…he moved swiftly from his chair, pressed the call-button, watched Erin rise from the rocker and head straight to the cot where she had left her veil and bra. He strode to the nursery door, opening it for the nanny to enter as fast as possible, waiting beside it. His heart was pummelling his chest. His hands clenched. The fight for control was so close to being a losing battle.

The nanny arrived.

Erin passed over Jack with the instruction, "He still needs to be burped." As soon as her hands were free, she grabbed her veil and bra. With her bodice still hanging down from her waist, she used the towel to cover her naked breasts, flashed her glowing rainbow smile at Peter, and said, "I'll get redressed in my suite."

Her suite.

Just along this hall, feet moving fast, Erin opening the door, flinging the wedding finery on the floor, turning to face him. He kicked the door shut. She was in his arms. He rubbed his cheek against the black silk of her hair, breathed in the heady scent of her. Her arms wound around his neck, pulling his head down. Their mouths met in a wild onslaught of needy kisses.

A break to catch their breaths.

"You've got too many clothes on, Peter," she said, excited eyes teasing his. "If you help me out of this wedding dress, I'll help you lose them."

A joyous laughter bubbled from him. He whipped her around, pulled the zipper down from her waist, pushed the skirt over her hips. She stepped out of it, looking incredibly sexy wearing white lace French knickers and a lacy garter belt attached to the fine silky stockings she wore. For a moment, his eyes feasted on the graceful curves of her back, the lush roundness of her bottom, her lovely long legs. Every muscle in his body was taut, screaming to leap into action. He couldn't wait for her to undress him.

His coat joined her clothes on the floor. His hands were tearing at his tie when she came to him, undoing his shirt buttons, fingers moving swiftly, unfastening his trousers. Neither of them cared about any sensual finesse in getting naked. This was not a journey of discovery. Urgency was uppermost. She wanted him. He wanted her. And the need to come together was a driving force that could not be contained.

He carried her to the bed. They sprawled on

it together. She wrapped her legs around him, lifting herself in wanton invitation for him to plunge straight into the sweet, warm depths of her.

He did.

"Yes-s-s-s," she cried out, the intensity of her pleasure coursing through him, making him wild to give her more.

They moved as one, rocking each other, pushing the excitement higher and higher. It was glorious. It was bliss. His woman, wanting him, needing him, loving him, giving herself with uninhibited passion and revelling in taking all he could give her. He felt the convulsive spasms and the gushing flow of her climax and plunged as deep as her arched body allowed, holding himself there, loving the sense of her melting around him.

Her hands stroked down his back, sliding over his buttocks, fingers digging in. "Go on, Peter," she urged. "I want to feel you come inside me."

He did.

Incredible ecstasy.

He kissed her, and her mouth was gentle and loving, her hands in his hair, tenderly caressing. They stayed entwined, joined as one, even when he rolled on his side, her head snuggled to the curve of his neck and shoulder. How long they lay in this contented intimacy he didn't know. Time was meaningless. He was happy simply to hold her, to know that she was happy, too.

"I guess we should be getting back to the marquee," she said on a rueful sigh.

He'd forgotten their wedding party.

Did it matter that they would be missed, guests commenting on their absence?

No.

Yet he and Erin had the rest of their lives to be together. Tonight was the night to show and share their happiness with everyone.

"Yes, we should," he decided. "I want to dance with you, Erin."

"I'd like that…our bridal dance."

He heard the smile in her voice.

It was okay to move.

They would be moving in unison again very soon.

The photograph released to the media the next day was of the bride and groom dancing. They were gazing into each other's eyes, smiling. No-one who looked at that photograph was in any doubt that Peter Ramsey and Erin Lavelle were happy with their marriage.

CHAPTER THIRTEEN

Los Angeles, fourteen months later...

THRONGS of fans waved and screamed from the roadside as the limousine rolled slowly forward in the long queue of limousines delivering stars of the big screen to the theatre where the Academy Awards ceremony was to be held. Erin remembered the same intense excitement flowing from the crowd of spectators who had turned up at the premiere of *The Mythical Horses of Mirrima,* four months ago.

It amazed her that so many people cared enough to wait hours to catch a glimpse of their favourite celebrities. Even children had nagged their parents into coming to see *her,* simply because she was the author of stories they loved. Before she'd married Peter, she'd hated feeling like a performing monkey in a zoo, but under his guidance, she'd learnt not to mind being stared at.

Just be yourself. Whatever buzz other people get out of seeing you doesn't have to touch what you are inside, Erin. Think of it as brightening their day. Like a rainbow. That's not a bad thing to do.

She'd even done a few interviews to promote the movie, managing them quite well because she'd followed his advice of saying only what she wanted to say and side-stepping the questions aimed at getting out of her personal stuff that she didn't want to give.

Take control away from them if it's not going the way you want.

Peter was so good at it. She'd learnt an enormous amount from him about how to deal with situations that had made her shrink inside herself or want to run away from in the past. Having him at her side made a huge difference. She wasn't alone. And he was an extremely intimidating protector—too big a man for anyone to get offside with him.

She remembered the conversation they'd had when he'd queried her decision to be reclusive—his wry comment, "Billionaires get to be performing monkeys, too. The difference between us, Erin, is that I've learnt to live with the zoo and not let it control me."

The criticism had stung. "I just don't like it, Peter. Being paraded around like a trophy, people sniping at you because you're lucky to be successful at what you do, and wanting you to give them *the formula* as though you can reduce your creativity to easily copied bits and pieces."

"But you like control," he'd replied seriously. "Withdrawing is the most negative form of it. Negative for you, too."

She hadn't liked his perception of her

decision not to court attention. It made her sound like a coward when what she'd been doing was avoiding the feeling of being a victim of other people's interests.

But he hadn't thought her cowardly. There'd been understanding in his eyes as he'd told her, "I was born to it, Erin. I had parents who taught me how to deal with it, how to let it flow past me and not let it tear at my sense of the person I am inside. I wasn't suddenly hit with celebrity status and all that goes with it the way you were. But if you let me help you, I can and will widen your world and make it easier for you to ride through all that you hide from so it doesn't affect anything that's really impor-tant to you."

Her prince…rescuing her from her ivory tower…and he had.

She turned to him now, smiling her apprecia-tion of the person he was, loving him.

He smiled back, gesturing to the window of

the limousine on his side of the passenger seat. "You're okay with this wild bunch of spectators? Not nervous?"

"It's a grand occasion. I don't mind them sharing it with us." She squeezed the hand that was holding hers. "Besides, I always feel okay when you're with me."

He laughed. "We definitely click on that point, my darling." His eyes simmered with desire as he added, "You're going to knock their eyes out when we walk the red carpet."

She laughed, perfectly happy to have been his *doll* this time. He'd insisted on having her dress especially designed and made for her— a gorgeous emerald-green satin gown, to which he'd added a fabulous emerald necklace with earrings to match.

"Thank you," she said. "You've made me look like a star."

"You are a star, Erin. Always will be to me."

She believed him. Everything he did for her

made her feel special, loved and cherished as she had always craved to be.

The limousine came to a halt. The door on Peter's side was opened.

"Showtime!" he tossed at her with a grin, and stepped out, ready to take her arm as she emerged from the back seat.

There was a sea of cameras, photographers yelling for their attention, television people wanting a quick on-the-spot interview. Erin smiled through it all.

They were ushered into the theatre to take their seats beside Zack Freeman and his lovely wife, Catherine, who were already there. Erin had become friends with both of them during the making of the film, and it was great to share the excitement of being here with them.

The people, the dresses, the amusing comments of the Master of Ceremonies, the thank-you speeches after each award was given out... Erin enjoyed all of it, though she couldn't stop her nerves from getting quivery when the nominations for Best Animated Movie were being read out.

Clips from each movie were shown and her heart swelled with pride as she watched hers— the warrior king of Mirrima, summoning his winged horses to rescue the men who'd been trapped by the evil enemy on a mountaintop. The horses looked fantastic, their gorgeous wings fully spread as they soared towards the mountain. It was a beautiful movie, and it would still be beautiful, even if the award went to one of the others.

"And the winner is…"

She held her breath.

"…*The Mythical Horses of Mirrima.* Creative director, Zack Freeman, producer, Peter Ramsey, author and screenplay writer, Erin Lavelle."

All three of them erupted from their seats in wild jubilation—hugs, kisses, excitement running rife. Erin was grateful she had the two men holding her arms in support as they walked to the stage. Her legs were shaking. Zack, who'd done it all before, accepted the award and made a lovely thank you speech, saying, with a nod of appreciation to her, that he'd been privileged to be given a great story, because without one, a great movie could not be made.

Someone in the audience started shouting, "Author, author…"

The cry was taken up around the whole theatre and the Master of Ceremonies beckoned her forward, offering her the microphone. Erin was paralysed.

"Go on" Peter urged.

"I haven't got anything prepared," she said in sheer panic at the thought of taking this huge spotlight with not only a glittering crowd of stars watching her, but probably millions of television viewers around the world, as well.

"Speak from your heart. You can't go

wrong," Peter assured her, giving her a gentle push forward.

Her feet somehow floated over to the podium. Her trembling hand managed to clutch the microphone. Her mind was in a frenzy, reciting, *Speak from your heart,* like a mantra.

"Thank you. Thank you very much," she said as she tried to find the right words. The audience quietened down and finally other words came to her. "It's a marvellous thing for an author to see her story come to life in such wonderful colour and movement, and for that I will always be grateful to Zack Freeman for his creative artistry. But most of all, I want to thank my husband, Peter Ramsey, who was the driving force behind making it happen. I haven't told him this, but while I was writing *The Mythical Horses of Mirrima,* he was very much in my mind and I based the character of the warrior king on what I thought of him. I love this movie…"

She turned and smiled at Peter. "…and I love this man, more than I can ever tell him. He is the king of my heart and always will be." Then she beamed at the audience, sending out a rainbow of love to everyone. "That's all I have to say."

The applause was deafening. She handed back the microphone and almost fled the stage with Peter hugging her tightly to his side. "And you're the queen of mine," he whispered in her ear as they made their way back to their seats.

She sighed, a blissful sigh of happiness.

Ever after, she thought.

She *would* have it with Peter.

They would both make it so.

MILLS & BOON PUBLISH EIGHT LARGE PRINT TITLES A MONTH. THESE ARE THE EIGHT TITLES FOR MARCH 2008.

THE BILLIONAIRE'S CAPTIVE BRIDE
Emma Darcy

BEDDED, OR WEDDED?
Julia James

THE BOSS'S CHRISTMAS BABY
Trish Morey

THE GREEK TYCOON'S UNWILLING WIFE
Kate Walker

WINTER ROSES
Diana Palmer

THE COWBOY'S CHRISTMAS PROPOSAL
Judy Christenberry

APPOINTMENT AT THE ALTAR
Jessica Hart

CARING FOR HIS BABY
Caroline Anderson

MILLS & BOON
Pure reading pleasure

0208 Rom LP